SMOKE TALK

Center Point
Large Print

Also by Nelson Nye and available from
Center Point Large Print:

The Killer of Cibecue
Wide Loop
Wildcats of Tonto Basin

**This Large Print Book carries the
Seal of Approval of N.A.V.H.**

SMOKE TALK

NELSON NYE

CENTER POINT LARGE PRINT
THORNDIKE, MAINE

1

Rambo thought of the things he'd been going to do before word of his sister had turned him south to eat up the miles in a killing rage. Two months ago that had been—two months yesterday—and the hate was still with him, but no longer the heat or that wild reckless fury. It was cold now and wicked, an inflexible purpose which had honed him down, carrying him up into these rock ribbed escarpments where the last sign had vanished like the sunerased snow.

He was a more patient man than had tracked into this country. He had stayed on quietly, taking a job with the Swallowfork outfit as cover for his presence, determined to hang and rattle till the fellow showed his hand. A man didn't lose himself in thin air like water. He was holed up here some place and sooner or later he would say or do something which would put Rambo onto him. He stood up in the oxbows, weight lightly resting against the swell of the saddle, and had his look around, still collecting landmarks against a time of need.

A vast and untamed country, this high land of the Superstitions; habitat of men who'd sloughed their pasts along with their scruples, rendezvous of those driven out of more settled places. All ups and downs, scary drops and difficult rangeland. Badlands on a gigantic scale, gouged and slashed by a thousand canyons and looking for all the world like some great cat had sharpened its claws here.

Outwardly, of course, the most of these fellows fell into some pattern of common acceptance, wearing the guise of honest men no matter what manner of lines marked their faces. He guessed that back of this pretense of belonging, however, predilections toward violence were held in check by threads only, threads which would snap in the first breath of danger. Wolves and coyotes. You knew what the wolves would do. It was the cowards you had to watch out for.

God's children, he thought, and shook his head in remembrance. He wondered what his folks must think if they could see him now, this Steve they had raised for the ministry. The edge of a twisted smile tugged his lips. What a man was born with was sometimes disciplined but seldom changed by prescription of rules laid down for conduct. He hadn't the temper or attitude—he knew this; he wasn't the forebearing sort. He'd been too much a man's kind of man for preaching, too quick to rile, too deplorably human.

Off there to the left, twenty miles across country and so small from this angle they looked like dolls' houses, were the headquarters buildings of

Swallowfork, a cow spread, second largest in the region using Post Oak for a supply depot.

Directly below him, partially hidden in the dust kicked up by hoofs and wagon wheels, he saw the roofs of town, a squalid collection of hit-or-miss carpentry, half constructed of logs and half clapboarded frames cowering behind their ridiculous false fronts like big dogs barking to keep fright away.

Beyond, ten miles by wagon rut, showed the squat brown adobes of Barred Circle headquarters. Barred Circle was the biggest ranch in this district, the far-flung property of a man who'd come early and taken all he wanted. During his life, if you put stock in legend, "Big Deke" Overpack—who'd come West from Louisiana—had held what he'd taken with an iron fist. He'd surrounded himself with a bunch of tough riders who regarded trespassers as rustlers and promptly swung them from the handiest limbs. Lesser men had stepped around Deke with considerable circumspection; but now he was gone, called aloft by his Maker, and the coyotes were yapping.

Rambo was glad his folks hadn't known about Della. It had been shock enough to them when, four years back, he had thrown up the Seminary, lit out for Colorado and taken a job skinning mules at Georgetown where silver was all but being picked up off the streets. He had given two years to that and eleven months to packing the tin at Golden before he'd rolled up his blankets and caught a slow freight for Texas.

Horses had always been in his blood and, with enough cash saved to get into the business, he'd been scouting around for a likely stallion when he'd heard about Della whom he'd set up at Pecos in a hat-making establishment.

He ground out his smoke on the horn of his saddle and picked up the reins, glancing again in the direction of Swallowfork. He was getting his beans and forty a month for holding down the southeast linecamp, but he guessed it would stick around long enough to let a fellow drag town smell through his system.

"Man doesn't live by bread alone," he reminded himself, easing the animal under him down the rushing headlong slope. He watched his mauve shadow dancing longer and longer ahead of him, but this wasn't all he watched. Though he sat the bay gelding with a loose-muscled slackness, a remote smile playing across the fold of his lips, there was an air of alertness in the way his cool glance absorbed all things about him.

He had a riding man's hips and broad shoulders; a leather-legged man with a spatter of dust buffly powdering assured features. He had blunt, capable fingers and black hair rebelliously curling below the shoved-back hat and blue-black jowls which no amount of scraping could turn the rich bronze of the rest of his angular highboned face. His hat was black, like his eyes, but it wasn't flat-crowned as the ones he'd worn earlier. There was just the suggestion of a twist to his nose and across his left temple the track of a scar, souvenirs of temper. These things, plus a small hoard of cash, were about all Steve Rambo could show for twenty-eight years of living. These and the unresolved conflict between instinct and training which, in unguarded moments, sometimes looked through his stare.

There wasn't a great deal to Post Oak. Nothing new. It was pretty much the same as half a hundred other towns Rambo had been through since turning his back on God's service. The street, in this first stain of twilight, lay deep in hoof-tracked yellow dust. The buildings hunkered along both sides had the tired resigned look of old men's faces. If they'd ever known paint it had long since gone, scoured away by the harsh sand-filled winds off the desert.

He passed a hoof-shaper's shop with its smell of cold iron and still-warm forge stink. Dust-fogged windows peered blankly through cobwebs and chinaberries and cottonwoods made an irregular line along the north walk. At intervals marked mostly by the spacing of saloons saddle horses stood hipshot and patient above the gnawed poles to which their users had hitched them, and a stable's aroma came through the wide opening beneath an unlighted lantern that was hung from its arch. Several men in tipped-back chairs were lazily whittling before the stage stop and he was aware of these eyeing him covertly.

He jogged on, guessing this to be a slack time around Post Oak, casually probing the town with his memory for detail. A hotel, on the right, had its row of still breeds with their backs hunched against the lattice-covered foundation; he could hear the clatter of dishes through open diningroom windows, the subdued murmur of conversation. A group of riders were loitering before the Silver Trinket's batwings, and three of them stared after him with fingers hovering nervously beside the sag of their cartridge belts.

A continuing smell of cooking brought him out of the saddle before the Cisco Cafe, and he was partway over the walk to its door when something glimpsed slanchways from the corners of his eyes wheeled him half around and hung him there, motionless.

There was the front and gaping doorway of a second stable across from him. There'd been nothing to notice when he'd got off his horse, but from where he stood now he could see inside its entrance the silhouettes of at least three persons stiffly standing above a dark something on the floor. He caught the pant of an angry breath and along the street several heads were turning. Three punchers in work-grimed Levi's coming out of the barber's shop stopped and Rambo, reminded this had nothing to do with him, was about to pull open the cafe's screen door when a girl's voice cried, "Get away from him, damn you—let him alone!"

2

Rambo saw the group of riders come off the Silver Trinket's porch, watched them start to cross the street and as abruptly freeze in their tracks. The three cowhands still stood before the barber shop, staring. People had stopped along both walks but none of them showed any intention of going nearer.

He was no more anxious to become involved than these others. He was in a strange town without authority from his range boss and had enough on his mind without taking chips in any deal embracing a woman.

Considering these facts he stepped across the dust quietly, disregarding the protests of common sense and past experience. He did, however, take the precaution of pulling his neck cloth up over the bridge of his nose before sliding into the gloom of the stable and, when he saw whom he'd braced and the nature of this business, was mighty thankful he had thought of it.

The group before him, at the moment, was too engrossed to note his arrival. The air was oppressive, fouled with the stench of horse urine and whiskey. It was a scene of revolting, stupifying brutality. On the floor amid straw and shreds of torn cloth two moaning, panting persons were entwined in desperate struggle. At one side of this turmoil a couple of men dressed as ranch hands confronted a girl who, by the look, was on the brink of hysteria. She was striving frantically to reach the struggling pair on the floor but the shorter fellow in range garb, brawny, bald-headed and with a face like a mastiff, grinning hugely was keeping her away from them. *"Faron—"* she kept crying, "Faron, stop it! Do you hear me?"

The one Rambo was looking at wouldn't be Faron. The hair was too long and it was black, not yellow. Black and fanned out around her shoulders like wet seaweed. She was fighting to get her hand up with a dismal, sobbing fury.

Baldhead pushed the blond girl back, his companion watching with a casual amusement. "Hell, it's only Injun Charley's whelp—she ain't got 'em all, either. Faron thinks—"

"Never mind," Rambo said. "Pull him off her, Anvil."

In the frozen quiet Steve could feel his heart pounding like a battery of stamp mills. The only sound in the place came off the floor as the man, panting hoarsely, tried to better his grip on the wrist with the knife. Anvil stood perfectly still, trapped with both fists much too far from his pistol; but the rage churning through him was so rank you could smell it.

13

Rambo tipped up his gunsnout. "I won't fool with you, Anvil. You heard me. Get at it."

Swallowfork's foreman licked dry lips. His eyes pried at Rambo. The other man stood rigid, arms above head, glance venomously unwinking as the orbs of a snake.

"You better light out of here, ma'am," Rambo said.

The yellow-haired girl never moved, never lifted her gaze off the pair on the floor. The pressure got tighter. The Swallowfork boss was so wild he was shaking. But, faced with the bore of that leveled sixshooter and those narrowed black eyes looking death at him over it, he knew better than to try out his luck right then. With a scowl he stooped and got both hands hooked under the top shape's shoulders.

"Hold it," Rambo drawled; and, to the girl: "Get his iron." He kept the other man covered while she did so.

When she was clear he nodded. Anvil spat and bent deeper and, with a grunt, bulged his muscles. When he threw his weight backward the man he had hold of was prized to his feet. Cursing and snarling, slobbering like a dog he tried to knock Anvil down but, with the man holding onto him, he couldn't get leverage.

The girl with the pistol said, "Faron!" sharply, futilely trying to get through to him; the other one sprang up and fled into the shadows.

"All right, turn him loose," Rambo thinly told Anvil. When the ramrod stepped back the drunken Faron peered round owlishly and then, gimpy legs uncontrollably folding, went down on his face. He didn't move but just lay there like a surfeited hog.

Rambo looked at the girl and saw reaction, deep within her, change the contours of her face. Disgust and pity were at war there and he thought for a moment she had reached the end of her string.

Then he saw her shoulders straighten. Like a dentist probing for unsound teeth she nudged the man's shape with the toe of her boot. Her chin came up. "Out cold," she said; and Rambo stared at her curiously.

"Your husband, ma'am?"

"Brother."

"You have far to go?"

"Ten miles."

Rambo thought about that. "If you'll go round up your horses I'll help you get him on one."

She looked at Faron again, and when the gloom had closed in behind her he considered his situation. He did not understand all he knew of this business but he grasped enough to see pretty plain he'd got into a thing which might have serious repercussions.

With his neckerchief over his face he didn't suppose these men suspected who had jumped them. He'd been careful with his voice and his garb held nothing distinctive. But if either of these fellows ever hooked him up with this deal it was plain as plowed grass he'd better keep away from Swallowfork. This might be Forko's shindy or it might be some foulness they'd cooked up on their own hook, but Anvil's face was set in unforgiving fury.

He said gruffly to the tall one, "Don't put no strain on your luck, Colorado, but reach down real gentle and unlatch that shell belt."

Rambo's use of his name brought no reaction from the man. He unbuckled the belt and let it slide down his legs, and only after it had settled behind his bootheels did Rambo catch the significance of why it had shucked to the floor with such quietness.

He looked hard at the man. "Now the gun," he said softly.

"What gun?"

"The one you've got stuck alongside your navel."

In Colorado's face he read his past and his future. It lay tucked between the tight-clamped lines ground into this tall one's enigmatic features; a threat and a promise of trouble to come.

Why, this fellow's a gunman! Rambo thought, startled. It seemed strange he hadn't become aware of this sooner. "You going to drop it," he

16

said, "or are you honing to reach for a harp and a halo?"

The purple blaze of a birthmark discolored the lower portion of the man's cold-jawed chin, and this now turned darker; but he lifted the gun and very carefully dropped it across a fold of the discarded belt. Rambo waited a moment and Colorado sneered.

"All right," Rambo said. "Now pick up that axe handle and let's see you wrap it around Anvil's bald head."

"Here—what's this?" Anvil bleated.

Anvil's gunman folded his arms and looked back at Rambo with an insolent assurance.

Rambo's gun barked, the sound whirling around between these walls like a mine blast. An involuntary yell came out of Colorado's throat and he grabbed a bleeding ear with a look of outrage shading toward recklessness.

"You want some more?" Rambo asked.

The man let go of his injured ear and, with a spate of foul language, caught up the axe handle. The Swallowfork boss squealing like a stuck pig flung himself to one side and took the blow on a shoulder. It slapped him flat against a wall down which he slid to the floor in a heap.

"Do a good job this time," Rambo said; and the axe handle put Anvil out for the count. Before Colorado could straighten, Rambo was upon him, clouting him back of the bloody ear with his pistol. Colorado struck the floor like a sack of dropped feed.

When the girl showed up with two horses in tow Rambo had both men bound and the wipe off of each wedged between their slack jaws. The girl glanced at them briefly without offering any comment. All her attention went to her brother.

The drunken Faron was raucously snoring. He was limp as a dishrag but Rambo got him wedged over a saddle and lashed feet and wrists underneath the horse's belly. He handed the girl the reins. "I reckon he'll lead all right that way."

"I don't know—" she began, but he waved her on out.

"I'm riding with you for a ways. We can do our gabbing later."

They rode without talk for the first couple miles, Rambo keeping both eyes peeled. He did considerable thinking along this stretch of road but without turning up any workable solutions. If that Swallowfork pair hadn't recognized him, to swap bases now would be the worst thing he could do. The smartest play, he thought, would be to go on back to his linecamp and act as though he'd never left it. He had got this far in his reflections when the girl finally broke her silence. "I don't know what to tell you or how to begin, but what you saw in that stable—"

"You got no call to tell me anything."

"But I can't have you thinking Faron's that kind of beast. He's not responsible—even less when he's been drinking; it's why they poured all that stuff down him. What you saw was . . . a glimpse of the devil that's in all men but which the most of you generally manage to keep hidden."

Rambo, turning that over through an interval of hoof sound, was finally moved to say, "Not a very charitable notion."

"What a woman thinks doesn't matter."

She handed that down like it was straight from Mount Sinai; and though Steve had himself quite frequently been of this opinion he considered it one of those things which, by and large, was best left unmentioned.

"All my life," she said abruptly, "far back as I can remember, I've lived in a man's world, balked by men's obstinacies, stepping around their prejudices, picking up after them and patching the pieces. Feuding—all the time fighting and feuding. Sometimes I could scream I get so all-fired fed up with it."

"Go ahead," he said; "get it out of your system."

He heard her draw a long breath. "I don't suppose I'm attractive. I've lived too long with violence. My father was a harsh, uncaring man who set himself up to be a king in this country and more or less got away with it. He ruined everything he touched. Faron, my brother, crawled into a shell; he was gentle, like Mother, naturally considerate and shy. I was cursed with an overabundance of energy but all Faron got was the tag-end of everything. Deke never spoke to him without intolerance or derision. He said I had all the spunk in the family. I got the boy's training. He left Faron home to do the house work and yard chores . . . until the men started noticing me. Then he left us both home."

"I guess you must be one of the Overpacks."

"That's right." She spoke bitterly. "The Barred Circle Overpacks. I'm the female, Lucie Anna."

"About Faron," Rambo said. "How do you mean he isn't responsible?"

"He isn't normal. He's been sick. About five years ago, belatedly, my father decided to make a man of him. The neighbors had all been brought to heel and, since he didn't want to have to leave the place to a girl and had nothing else to occupy his time, he made out to teach Faron the things he should have learned as a boy. First lesson was horses; he turned Faron loose with the rough string and one of those broncs kicked my brother in the head. He hasn't ever got over it."

"What I saw in that stable looked a little rough for horseplay."

"It wasn't horseplay. It was vicious, malicious and deliberate, another in a long string of liquor-inflamed incidents designed to stir up trouble. Someone's always giving him whiskey; they know he can't resist it—will do anything after he's had a drink."

She eyed him again. "You're thinking I should have left him at home, but I had to come in and I didn't dare leave him. Besides a crippled-up old wagon boss who cooks for the outfit, we've only got three hands and Gerry—he's our ramrod—keeps them out on the range."

Rambo said, suddenly curious, "A big spread like yours, running short-handed, is a kind of natural target for people packing grudges."

"Do you think I don't know that?"

"If this thing's following a pattern you must have some idea—"

"I have a lot of ideas but I haven't the means of backing any of them up."

"Sell off some of your land."

"I can afford to pay wages; there's more to it than that. Would *you* take a job with Barred Circle?"

"I've got a job now."

"So have most of the men who are worth taking on. Those who don't have jobs, I'm given to understand, would be embarrassed to take pay from a woman; that may be part of what I'm up against. Barred Circle has the rep of being a bad spread to work for. Things happen to their hands. Sometimes those things turn out to be serious."

Rambo looked at her sharply. "You mean . . . ?"

"What I said. We've had three men bush-whacked in less than two months."

Rambo soundlessly whistled. "What's the matter with the sheriff?"

"He's not completely a fool."

They rode another mile and, abruptly drawing rein, the girl swung down and put her head to the ground. When she was back in her saddle she said, "I can make it all right now. It's not too much farther."

"I don't mind going the route."

"It's good of you to offer. But we're not being followed. You've done enough for us now." She held out her hand.

Rambo found it cool and firm. "If you ever change your mind," she said, "or feel like working for a petticoat, there'll be a place to hang your hat at Barred Circle."

"But that's just it," Rambo declared as she took back her hand, "if I don't go with you now I'll probably never be able to find it."

Her shape was still for a moment and then a little laugh came out of her. He found it pleasant and enormously surprising, yet it provoked a sudden anger. He had gone without his supper, risked the wreck of his plans for this girl, and he thought a laugh was damned poor return until he realized it was the girl herself, and his own reactions to her, which had brought this anger up in him. He knew then why he wanted to go on to the ranch with her and if he'd had it to do over he'd have taken the words back. He'd come into this country to kill a man. There was no place in his plans for a woman.

It was still a good hour short of moonrise when they arrived at Barred Circle. About all he could see was the vague shapes of dark buildings. Horses nickered in a corral and a dog barked off yonder and came bounding toward them and the girl said, "Down, Rover!" as they pulled up by a porch; and Rambo stepped out of the saddle. The dog kept its distance, still growling.

The girl swung down lightly and called the dog to her. "I'll get a lamp lit," she said over her shoulder. Her spurs crossed the porch and a door was pushed open and the dog growled again as Rambo stepped back to Faron. The man was still drunk, still out and still reeking of whiskey.

Rambo untied him, got him over a shoulder and, as a light sprang up, stepped onto the porch with him. The girl called, "In here," and he followed her into a room off the kitchen, the still-growling dog padding after them.

She set the lamp on a chest of drawers and Rambo lowered Faron's inert weight to a bed. He had the girl's yellow hair and a ragged moustache and, even breathing through his mouth, he wasn't half bad-looking in a slack-jawed sort of way.

Rambo straightened. "You want me to get the clothes off him?"

"If you don't mind," she said and, to the dog, "Behave, Rover," and went back to the kitchen. He heard her lifting off stove lids and poking up the fire.

Rambo glanced at the dog. It was a big German shepherd, watching him intently with its hackles still lifted and black lips drawn back off its gleaming white fangs. "Come," Rambo said, "let's make up."

The dog neared him cautiously and sniffed of his fingers, yellow eyes bright and watchful. Then it nosed the leather chaps and shirt and, finally, his face. It wagged its tail a couple times and Rambo, considering this a truce, began to get Faron out of his clothing.

When he returned to the kitchen the dog padded along beside him. A pot on the stove was beginning to make coffee smell and a skillet was filled with eggs and strips of spattering bacon. "You'll find a place to wash on the bench outside the door."

"Expect I'd better—"

"Nonsense," she said, smiling over her shoulder. "You'll not go without eating—hurry up! It's about ready."

Rambo washed and ran fingers through his rebellious black hair. She was all he'd reckoned and a heap more besides. She indicated Anvil's gun on the table. "You'd better take that along."

She was pretty as a basket of chips, Rambo thought.

Lithe, she was, and full-bodied. Her yellow hair was the color of wheat straw and her eyes reminded him of mountain pools, indefinably blue, filled with hidden depths and meanings. She was tall for a girl but not too tall, very pleasing in that blue riding skirt pulled tight across hips with a wide leather belt. The tips of impertinent breasts pushed against the cloth of the round-necked white shirtwaist she wore, and he liked the look of her long-fingered hands as she scooped eggs and bacon out onto their plates. She fetched the coffeepot then and crisp brown toast and they sat down, the dog sitting near with ears pricked, eyes expectant.

The girl looked more relaxed now, body graceful and careless; he mused how it might be to sit across from her each evening, and was disturbed by such thoughts, by the intimacies conjured. This girl was real and not ashamed to show her interest.

The food was good and he ate steadily but didn't take much pleasure from it. He knew it had been a mistake to come here. The girl was too close and he was too much aware of the unspoken notions vibrating between them. He washed down the last mouthful with the dregs of his coffee.

"You'll want to smoke," she said smiling as he was shoving his chair back; but he shook his head, knowing that even more he needed to get away from here, from the demands which her nearness was calling up inside of him.

He got to his feet and she rose also and he bent over and got his hat. "I'm obliged to you, ma'am, but I expect I'll have to—" He broke off as the dog, softly growling, swung round to face the door.

Over the yard a moment later swept the sound of hurrying hoofbeats, faint at first but rapidly swelling.

"Kill that light," he said bleakly and, when he reckoned he could see, pulled open the door. The dog went out with a rush. Horse sound quit and beyond the porch a man said, "All right, boy," and then, louder: "Jay Allison."

The girl touched Rambo's arm. "Come up, Jay."

"Who's that with you?"

"A friend—"

"Then get the lamp lit so I can have a look at him."

"No lamp," Rambo said, and saw the man's shape duck back of his horse and remain there, coldly still, through a space of pounding heart-beats, abruptly growling in a voice grown brittle with suspicion: "What do they call you?"

"Would there be a word better than 'friend' in your language?"

"In my book friends ain't afraid to be seen."

Rambo heard the rasp of steel against leather and knew the fellow had a gun up. But the girl kept hold of Rambo's arm. "Listen, Jay—"

"For all I know he's got a knife at your ribs."

She said angrily, "Don't be silly! I said he was a friend—"

"Then what's he scared of the light for?"

"There was trouble in town. This man got us out of it. But he had his face covered; he's got a job—"

"Who's he with?"

Rambo, not liking this, reluctantly said, "Swallowfork."

The stillness turned ugly. The girl took her hand away. The man in the yard said, "Them sons of bitches!" and "I'll stay where I'm at until he gets the hell outa there."

3

From his built-up carefully acquired knowledge of this country Rambo was able to bypass town, thus appreciably reducing the weary miles he must travel to get back to his post at the Swallow-fork linecamp. He rode steadily, pushing the bay at first between a lope and a gallop, but as his thinking took over more and more of his attention the gelding picked its own pace and thereafter frequently soldiered.

The moon came up, bathing the range in blues and silver, but Rambo had no eye for the grandeur of this beauty. Coyotes lifted their voices now and again from the yonder ridgetops, that lonely chorus a fitting backdrop for reflections revolving about the girl at Barred Circle. He thought of Anvil James and the gun hawk, Colorado, of Lucie Anna's brother and of the ugliness encountered in that Post Oak stable. But mostly he thought of the girl and the mission which had fetched him into this high hill country. Save for that he wouldn't have met her, yet because of it how could he admit her attraction or hope to carry their acquaintance further?

No man whose intentions held a pretense of decency would seek to involve a girl in any sequence whose outcome was preordained to be murder. He'd never considered it in this light, looking on it as retribution; but with Lucie Anna on his mind the act took shape in sharpest clarity and he saw that murder was what he'd planned. Sure, he'd intended to give the man first bite, back him into a corner where he'd no choice but draw—this to take care of the legal aspects and clear his skirts of responsibility for the killing.

An old dodge, this business of ridding one's self of an enemy under the fiction of firing in self-defense; as old as the West, as hallowed by tradition as the gun fighter's walk down the center of a road. With that girl on his mind Rambo couldn't defend it. He knew very little of the man he was after but he didn't think it likely the fellow could be as apt with a pistol as himself who had packed the star during the eleven roughest months in the history of a boom town.

Had Rambo shot the man at once—and he would if he could have found him—he would not have considered himself at all culpable in spite of the years he had spent studying Gospel. No matter what God thought about it the West accorded a man the right to kill his own snakes, and this would still be snake stomping. Only now it was become a cold-blooded proposition, not something done in a passion but something planned and deliberate, a thing steeped in cold hatred which went square against God.

Rambo scowled through the moonlight. He'd put the woman out of mind; he certainly owed that much to Della. If he hadn't gone traipsing off after horses the thing wouldn't have happened. It was his responsibility and, by the Prophets, he'd take care of it. He would do what he had come here to do and keep away from Barred Circle. Which was none of his business anyway. He was no Don Quixote to be tilting at windmills; and none but a fool or some damn callow kid would crawl out on a limb for a girl he hadn't known but for the space of two hours. Love? Rambo laughed, and then he snarled in rebellion.

It was close to four o'clock when he came round the last hill and looked down on the lineshack he was supposed to be staked out at. He was considerably surprised to mark a gleam of light from the cabin; he'd pulled away from here yesterday in the shank of the morning and there had been no occasion to have a lamp lit then.

He stopped his bay gelding in the darkness of box elders and probed the cabin's environs with sharply suspicious eyes. The extra horses of his own string were still penned in the corral but there were three additional animals on trailing reins at one side of the open doorway and a mumble of muted voices came drifting up to him faintly. Who were these fellows and what did they want? Were they strangers or men from the outfit's headquarters? If the latter, what had fetched them?

He could find out quick enough by going down there but he wasn't quite ready to do anything that precarious. Any ordinary message meant for him from the home place would have come in the daytime and been fetched by one man. Had such a message come yesterday it would have been scribbled on paper and the man wouldn't have stayed—not all this time. Too, the grouping of the horses proved these men were together, had arrived as one unit. Whether strangers or a part of the Swallowfork outfit, their presence here at this time was bound to mean trouble. It was the unknown nature of this trouble which urged Rambo to caution.

Several choices of action were open to him. He could ride off undiscovered. He could go down there. He could, still hidden, announce his presence. He could wait where he was for further developments and/or proof of their identity.

He debated these choices for another several moments, eyes narrowed and watchful as he carefully examined their various angles and, one by one, discarded them. This linecamp was his responsibility to Swallowfork and he could not with clear conscience repeat his earlier performance and simply ride away from it; he must gain some inkling of who was down there and why. This much he owed Swallowfork.

He backed his horse out of the trees and rode him back around an outcrop of sandstone and mountain mahogany and there got out of the saddle. He tied the bay securely and got his Winchester from its scabbard beneath the stirrup fender. And stood another moment, thinking.

He went back to the trees and went through them on his belly, very slow and with due care, until he could look over the rim of the ridge and see again that lighted doorway. To his left, and well within this spindling growth's shadows, were a number of boulders, big around as washtubs, firmly embedded in the shale of this slope. He wriggled over to where they would serve as a breastwork and lay there awhile, watching the cabin from between them, silently cursing the chill which was steadily becoming more acute as dawn neared.

He had hoped to wait out these men's reappearance, but now he saw something which convinced him he couldn't afford to. A low ground fog was rolling up from the bottoms, beginning to stir like smoke all across the face of the pocket. In another quarter hour as Rambo knew from experience, the whole lower half of that cabin would be blanketed.

He was probably as much as fifty feet above the place and not much over a hundred yards away when he settled the Winchester's stock against his shoulder, lined his sights on the doorway and squeezed off his first message.

Nothing happened. No one shouted. The only reply was the snort of a horse. He could see where the bullet struck by the dust and put a second one over it and, with the echoes caterwauling off the shaley slopes, heard a pan jump and clatter as the lamp went out.

He fired three shots in swift succession, sending the first and third, to the best of his judgment, through the glass of the nearest window. He could see two sides of the cabin and each of these sides held one of its two windows. He put another slug through that still-yawning doorway, only the top four-fifths of which was now to be seen above the creep of the fog. Not taking any chances then, he rolled three feet to the left and reloaded.

He heard the slam of the door and took a quick glance but, not discovering any movement, concluded he had them bottled. Both windows blossomed with muzzle flare and he dug his face down into the ground while blue whistlers cut twigs from the branches above him. He risked another quick shot and scrounched like a lizard when a slug ricocheted off the flank of the nearest boulder.

Bits of kicked-up dirt rattled across the back of his brush jacket as he squirmed to his former vantage and cautiously thrust his rifle's barrel between rocks. His second shot fetched down the stovepipe, but the fog was now lapping the sills of the windows and he knew before dawn, unless a wind came along, the whole place would be lost in it.

Red tongues of flame lanced from both of the windows and the air screamed around him, driving him flat against the ground. A high-powered saddle gun started banging to the west of him; and Rambo realized then that one of those men had gotten out. Bits of shale and clots of earth spattered against the left side of his hat and jacket and sweat cracked through the pores of his skin.

He came around on his belly and fired at the flashes. When they quit with no yell he guessed the man was changing places, and he backed deeper into the trees and got a good solid rock between himself and the general direction from which the saddle gun had spoken. He couldn't see the cabin windows now and suddenly he decided it was time to get out of there.

The man above him opened up again, hammering the trees with his screeching pellets, shaking a rain of bark and twigs from the branches. Rambo kept low while he counted the concussions, and when the count showed the gun was empty he drove up off his knees and made a run for his horse, pulling up just short of it in the lee of the outcrop. He squirmed up under the mountain mahogany and crouched there, breathing raggedly, with his pull-finger curled about the trigger of his rifle.

In a moment, above his heart-pound, he caught the thud of running boots. Nostrils flared, eyes scrinched to glittering slits, Rambo waited with baleful patience for the man to put in an appearance.

The light from the moon had gotten thin now and feeble with the shadows all streaky and nothing none too clear. He guessed the false dawn was lifting its grays behind the eastern mountains, but he kept his attention quartering over the slope.

He caught no blur of motion. No sound out there at all; but somewhere, in the blue-black stain of fringing timber, the fellow with that high-powered saddle gun was waiting, just as Rambo waited, for something to throw his lead at.

Nor would that pair at the cabin very long remain idle. Even now they might be moving up back of him, crawling and creeping through the brush and low bushes to cut him off from his horse and flush him into the open where their friend in the timber could get a clear crack at him.

Rambo bitterly decided he hadn't been extremely smart. Instead of showing improvement it was plain his situation was by the moment growing more desperate.

Decidedly uncomfortable, he turned his head

about, peering back of him. The only live thing he could locate was the vague blotch of his bay gelding in that clump of squatting cedars forty paces to the rear. Might as well have been forty miles, he thought, for all the good the horse was to him there.

He brought his head front again, cold as a well chain when stiff leaves just above him scraped the crown of his hat. He crouched rigid, scarce breathing, still hearing the rasp of that sound through this stillness, feeling as exposed as a steer in a branding chute.

His alarm had barely subsided when, with his eyes grimly cruising the timber, he caught the tag-end of a definite motion. Even as he stared a shape detached itself from the shadows. Before he could get his Winchester up two shots slammed racket in simultaneous explosions, one behind, the other above him. The man who'd stepped out of the timber crumpled.

"Got him, by grannies!" cried the fellow above Rambo, pushing exultantly forward across the open slope. He made a first rate target but not daring to fire—or even turn, for that matter—Rambo heard the man back of him come out of the brush, and the oncoming tramp of his footfalls approaching. This second sniper moved around Rambo's concealment with the reins of Rambo's gelding firmly clasped in one fist, a still-smoking rifle protruding grimly from the other; and not until that moment was Rambo finally convinced of their identity.

There could be no mistaking that gaunt, raw-boned shape with the chin straps dangling below the cold-jawed face. This was the gunhawk, Colorado, and the one cutting across the slope was Anvil, the Swallowfork ramrod. Rambo was sure of it when the man yelled impatiently, "C'mon, Brick, I got him—no need you hidin' out any longer. Slip down and fetch up them hosses."

Brick, Rambo reckoned, would be the man who'd stepped into their fire from the timber. He wasn't in shape to slip anywhere. But, until Anvil reached him, Anvil wouldn't know that and Rambo, doubling for him, might at least get as far as the penned broncs by the lineshack.

Getting out of that mahogany he was mightily tempted. Main reason he didn't try it was the conviction, if he did, he'd have these fellows on his trail till he got quit of this country, laying for him, crowding his play at every turn. But if he could shove a bluff at them right now and make it stick he'd be free to hunt his snake without too much further interference.

On the strength of this belief, his Winchester gripped in the crook of an elbow, he tramped after the gunhawk, keeping about ten paces behind his own led horse.

The light was pretty poor now, the flaccid

moon a dim gray disk, the eastern sawtops black against a reef of leaden cloud that looked like a rumpled sheet thrust back of them—one that had been used about six months by a sheepherder.

Rambo wasn't worried too much about the gunhawk seeing him. At forty feet, in this kind of gloom, you couldn't tell friend from foe without a spyglass. But Colorado never turned. He came up to the edge of timber hardly three strides back of the Swallowfork boss, the gelding concealing Rambo's presence from the latter.

Anvil, bent above the recumbent shape, was reaching down to shift it when he suddenly snatched his arm back and turned rigid, raggedly breathing.

Colorado, slouching to a stop, inquired, "Vinegarroon or orange wriggler?"

For a moment the ramrod seemed not to have heard, and then his short and squat shape came around like a sidewinder and he cried with an outraged snarl of fury: "You dumb son of a bitch—you've shot the wrong man!"

4

"The wrong man!" gasped Colorado, and was twisting his head, trying to see around Anvil, when Rambo stepped clear of the gelding's dark bulk.

"Were you boys laying for me?"

The gun fighter's jaw dropped. His boss didn't appear to like the looks of that rifle. He said, "Let's not git upset now," and swallowed a couple of times kind of dry like. Then he recalled who he was and the prestige properly due him for rodding this outfit, and managed to say gruffly, "What the hell would we want to be layin' fer you for?"

"That's what I've been wondering ever since you rode up."

"You knowed we was here?"

"You made enough racket for a blind man to know it, though I could tell you wasn't figuring to sound much louder than spiders—"

"If you was here why didn't you say so?"

"I cut my teeth before I tackled long pants," Rambo drawled and, eyes brightly narrow, considered them a spell while the gun fighter glowered and the Swallowfork boss shifted his weight about uneasily. "Mostly," Rambo said, "I like to let a man deal his own game—up to the point, anyways, where he begins to find it convenient to supplement his cards with iron."

"Hell," Anvil said, resorting to bluster, "you shot first!"

"I generally aim to," Rambo nodded. "I've found shooting first is a pretty good idea when a feller's on a spread that's working sand eels. Now suppose you answer my question."

"I already told you—"

"Sure. But what you told and what you did don't appear to have much in common. Try again. This time never mind the embroidery."

The range boss's cheeks, in this brightening light, showed about as sociable as a pulque-drunk squaw's, but he managed to bottle most of what he felt inside him. He was caught flat-footed with a corpse on his hands and no one but a fool would ever ascribe the cause to accident. He licked his lips. He said, "To tell you the truth, we come over here lookin' for rustlers—"

"You figured to find them using my cabin?"

"The whole damn place was so quiet—"

"It's most generally pretty calm about the time of night you got here." Rambo looked at Colorado. "You want to try your jaw for a spell?"

"Well, it's like Anvil said. We figured mebby them skunks had jumped you an' had you tied up in the shack there—"

"And you were lifting and putting your feet

down so quiet account of you didn't want to wake me? That sounds like the truth." Rambo's teeth gleamed at Anvil. "So when you finally made sure I wasn't in the shack you sat down, thinking maybe you'd better wait a bit for me; and when I tossed a few chunks of lead at the place you figured it was the rustlers—"

"You can laugh," Anvil glowered, "but by God there *is* rustlers!"

"So when you saw poor old Brick there stepping out of these trees you figured he was one of them and—"

Goaded past containment now the range boss, flinging aside his caution, cried, "We figured he was *you!*" A murderous, almost maniacal fury blazed out of his glaring hate-congested features. "An' if you don't dig for the tules we'll git you yet!"

"Well, at least we know where we stand now, don't we?"

Rambo's cool indifference appeared to puzzle the man and he made a visible effort to get hold of himself. Some of the ruddy color drifted out of his cheeks and something crossed his face like doubt. "You claimin' you been at this camp all night?"

"Where'd you reckon I'd been?"

"Why wasn't you in the cabin?"

Rambo's laugh held contempt. "You sent me over here to take care of the stock. When a man hears a calf start bawling in the night—"

"What time was that?"

"I never looked at a clock. You told me this was a twenty-four hour job."

He saw the two men exchange glances. "What'd you find?"

"I didn't find anything. Now what's this all about, if you don't mind a poor dumb cowpuncher asking?"

Anvil wasn't satisfied but he was still enough uncertain, and enough plagued by worries over the complications presented by Brick, that he could say with gruff belligerence, "We run into a little unpleasantness in town an' the idea come to us you mighta had a hand in it."

"Me? In town? Putting the skids under you two?" Rambo asked, derisively snorting, "Do I look like a chump?"

Colorado, with no capacity for civility, said: "You look like the kind that'd give his shirt to a filly."

"Filly—you mean calico?" Rambo peered at them, thoughtful. "So there was a woman mixed up in it." He let curiosity creep into his stare, finally grinning like he found the notion pretty hard to swallow. "Which one of you sports played Romeo?"

"Never mind," Anvil growled, getting red in the face again. "You goin' to keep that thing pointed at us all day?"

Rambo seemed surprised to learn they'd imagined it was deliberate. "Shucks, I doubt if the thing's even loaded," he said, hunching the butt to his shoulder and carelessly squinting down its barrel at Colorado. He poked a finger over the trigger.

The gun fighter's eyes looked like they'd roll off his cheekbones. Gray as a floormop he cried, almost beside himself: "Man—for Chrissake don't pull that!"

Rambo lowered the Winchester. Colorado's knees began to shake. Sweat stood out on his cheeks like raindrops and the lump in his throat went up and down like a broken piston. Even Anvil seemed a little pale around the gills.

Rambo appeared not to notice. Taking the gelding's reins from Colorado's limp grasp he swung into the saddle and scabbarded his rifle quite as though he were insensible to the rip-tide gusts of feeling which were curling through the rose-stained glow of the dawn just about to break over the horizon. Only for so long as he could keep this pair off balance, gouged and prodded by the continuing leap of alternate doubts and fears, did he see much chance for getting out of this alive.

He could not shoot them out of hand as they'd shot Brick and would shoot him if he took one false step or gave them time for any clear thinking. He couldn't afford to even nick them unless he cared to remain in this country a marked man, subject to continual threat of reprisal, forced to carry on a running war with them, armed as they might very well be with all the resources of Swallowfork. He could not chance that with any hope of finding the man he'd come looking for. He was like a man in a nightmare walking a tightrope while someone assiduously sawed the far end.

But none of this thinking leached through Rambo's expression; he appeared entirely unmindful of the black looks they gave him. When Anvil suggested packing the dead man on the gelding, Rambo said, "This bronc's too skittish—can't stand the smell of blood. Anyways, Brick ain't my problem. What are you figuring to do about him?"

"Never mind," Anvil growled. "Since he ain't your problem what you don't know won't hurt you."

"I don't want him buried around here," Rambo said.

The ramrod's face tightened up and Colorado, still gray cheeked, ground his molars in rageful silence. It was plain he was minded to put hand to pistol but Rambo's indifference must have discouraged the notion, or maybe it was the look Anvil gave him. "Colorado," Anvil said, "you can fetch up our horses."

There was a skeptical slant to Rambo's thin

smile. "Apt to take him quite a while the way they scattered during that shooting. Maybe we'd better all go back and you and me will look for the horses while Colorado gets some grub on the table. How would that be?"

The blaze on the gun fighter's chin darkened angrily. "I didn't hire out to be no damn pot wrangler!"

Rambo shrugged. "Fellow never knows what he can do until he tries it. We can't ask Anvil to demean himself with cooking, and I'm not turning my back after that crack he made awhile ago. With Brick here showing what carelessness will do—"

"Hell, you don't want to hold that against me." Anvil choused a parched smile across his bald cold-jawed mouth. "I was feelin' kind of worked up then—I didn't mean nothin' by it."

Rambo, nodding like he took this for gospel, said, "But accidents will happen."

"Brick just stepped into a little tough luck. Mighta happened to anyone—"

"I don't want it to happen to me," Rambo said; and Anvil peeled back his lips in a ghastly cackle.

"Come on," he said, "let's git down to the shack. We're all in this together. I'll tell Forko Fox we was chasin' them rustlers an'—"

"What rustlers?"

Anvil's testy look faded into a wink. "Cripes, we always got rustlers; it's the Ol' Man's favorite topic. So we was chasin' these fellers an' one of 'em opened up an' poor ol' Brick went an' caught the whole load."

"That's going to be the story, eh?"

"Sure. We'll fetch him back to the ranch an' do it up right. Give him a reg'lar plantin' with a prayerbook an' everything."

"That ought to make everything jake with him," Rambo said. "I'll ride along and make sure you don't leave out none of the fine points."

Anvil, stopped before the cabin, wheeled his head around, blackly glaring. "Who the hell do you think is goin' to watch this range?"

"It's been here quite a spell and ain't got lost yet that I notice. If you're scared somebody'll beef a cow you can leave Colorado—"

"Wouldn't that look cute!"

"I don't care how it looks," Rambo said, "but I'm going to be on hand when you tell Fox about Brick's killing."

5

Anvil's face was baked dark skin with no expression on it. But the eyes were something else again. Like glinting flakes of chipped obsidian they glared snakily out of his flung-back head, hurling the full blast of his frustrated temper at the man on the gelding who looked maddeningly back at him with a degree of tranquillity he must have found insufferable.

Now a grin loosed the gleam of Rambo's hard white teeth. "Don't think," he said softly, "you're going to pin that on me."

It was, strangely, Colorado who stepped into the breach. He said, "Them's my sentiments exactly," and the silence stretched out thin and tough while the sun rocked across the granite crags of the mountains and set gold fire to the rims of these slopes.

Anvil said, "Mister Fox won't like it—" but the gun fighter snorted. "He damn sure ain't goin' to fire all three of us!"

In the end, putting the best face he could on it, Anvil nodded. But it was not to be imagined giving in this way pleased him; it was a thing impelled by weight of numbers, by the gun fighter's decision to back Rambo's stand. It was

Anvil's own fault for letting temper usurp the function of judgment, forgetting in that brief moment that Colorado, being a mercenary, never put trust in anyone.

So the Swallowfork boss merely nodded, storing his spleen against a time more propitious. The rifle in his hands was too cumbersome and awkward, no good at close quarters against two men armed with belt guns. After being cut loose in that Post Oak stable he hadn't been able to find his own pistol; the Overpack girl had apparently gone off with it and his head hurt too much for him to think straight right now or this Rambo never would have got the upper hand of him. And that was something else to nourish— the remembrance of Colorado swinging that axe handle.

The morning was pretty well shot by the time they caught sight of Swallowfork headquarters. They'd been riding the hills for the past three hours with the ascending sun beating down ever warmer. Now a thousand feet ahead the trees gave out again and so did this high land, sloping gently downward into a platterlike basin through which a creek meandered, passing out over solid rock beneath a kind of natural portal like the pictures Steve had seen of the Rainbow Bridge in Utah. The trail led under this vast stone arch and, beyond it, dark against this new growth of grass, he saw again the rambling shape of the big one-storey ranch house, the bunkhouse and harness shed and the two-storey barn. Pole corrals were fetched to notice by the whickering of penned saddle stock. A lazy curl of blue-gray smoke funnelled thinly up from the cookshack stovepipe where Dirty Shirt, the Swallowfork cook, would be fixing chuck for himself and the owner; all the hands of course, kept over from fall roundup, being out on the range.

"He's goin' to think," Anvil growled, "it's goddam funny it took three growed men to bring home one dead one." He glanced at them covertly from the corners of his eyes. "You boys can take Brick on over to the bunkhouse—"

"I guess not," Rambo said. "I don't like to wear out my welcome but, until this business of Brick gets settled, I expect to hang and rattle right along with you."

"That goes double," Colorado nodded.

Anvil said no more till they pulled up before the house. He got disgustedly out of the saddle and dragged his spurs across the porch and grimly rapped on the casing at one side of the door. "If you're inside, Mister Fox, I'd like fer you to step out here."

They heard his weight cross the floor and the screen door opened and he came onto the porch, a slender and darkly handsome man whose quick eyes took in the whole scene at one glance, pausing longest on Rambo and then coming around without remark to Anvil's face.

The range boss cleared his throat. "Brick, here," he said, "stepped into a little trouble over at the southeast linecamp about a hour short of daylight."

"Looks like he stopped a couple of bullets."

"Yeah. He did. You remember tellin' me last week you wanted a check of the linecamps? Shenk, at Camp Two, told me yesterday he'd seen skulkers workin' through the pines north of his place twice in the past several days. Both times these fellers slipped their picket pins before he could git close enough to mug 'em. We quit his camp around four yesterday, aimin' fer Rambo's. Right after dark we smelled dust an' caught hoof sound—Brick thought once or twice he heard cattle bawlin'. Rustlers, we figured, an' spread out, thinkin' to catch 'em, cold turkey, afore they knowed what had hit 'em. But them sorry sons was—"

"How much beef did they get away with?"

"That's what's got me stopped. We looked around some this mornin'. We found sign where they'd thrown a little jag of steers together. We seen where they cut south but the cows wasn't with 'em. They musta just turned 'em loose an' dug fer the hills when we lit into them."

The Swallowfork owner took a long look at Rambo. "What are you doing here?"

50

"I dragged along for the ride."

A dark flush touched the ranchman's spare cheeks but he didn't swell up the way Anvil had looked for. He got a cigar from a little silver case and bit the end off. "Were you at the linecamp?"

"Where would you reckon I was?"

Fox's jaw came up and his brows pulled down and an expectant grin tugged the corners of Anvil's mouth, but again the anticipated explosion didn't materialize. The range boss felt cheated when the ranch owner said with an unreadable expression, "I've never got in the habit of playing guessing games with cowhands. Were you at that cabin or weren't you?"

"I wasn't far away."

"Did you hear the shooting?"

"I heard the whistle of lead, too," Rambo said, nodding.

Something sharp peered out of Fox's brightening glance and he bent the edge of this stare across Anvil. Bringing it back he said testily, "Get down, man, where I can do my talking without having to put my neck out of joint."

If Rambo paused before complying with this order the hesitation was so brief as to pass unremarked. But not even the crustiness of rugged individualism could account for a man getting off the wrong side of his horse. Nothing but reluctance toward exposing his back could explain doing that, and such distrust bred swift reaction.

Colorado's muddy eyes turned darker. The range boss sneered and the Swallowfork owner, twisting the cigar across his teeth, gave the new hand the benefit of an extremely fishy regard. He looked again at Anvil's holster, rasped the return of this glance across the gun fighter's scowl and, stepping back, watched all three of them. "So you heard the screech of lead."

"Ride out," Rambo grinned at the range boss's discomfiture, "and take a look at that cabin."

Fox said to Colorado, "How far from the line-shack did you tie into those rustlers?"

The gun fighter's glance thrust the question at Anvil. Fox's cheeks pulled thinner, molding the bones of his face, and the range boss, licking dry lips, said tightly, "About two miles," and then, with a wind in his chest and his teeth almost shut: "they had to larrup right past it gettin' away from our guns. With him runnin' out they'd nacherally throw a few slugs. He's goddam lucky he wasn't fixed like Brick!"

"All right," Fox nodded. "Put someone else at Camp Three—"

"Now, Mister Fox, I dunno's I'd—I mean I got no business buttin' acrosswise of you this way, but . . . Hell, you ain't fixin' to fire him, are you?"

"You don't think I should?"

"I'd be inclined to give him another chance," Anvil answered, making out not to notice Colorado's dropped jaw. "He's a bit-champer

52

sure enough an' shows a heap longer on guts than sense, but he seems to have the makin's of a pretty fair hand. It's gettin' along towards roundup now—"

"Well, I'll see," the rancher said. "You boys go on and get Brick fixed up. Rambo, step into my office."

6

Rambo didn't care for any part of what he'd got into. He was like a man walking blindfold about the edge of a boghole, scared almost to put his foot down. Sure, he'd thrown the hooks into Anvil, curious to observe the man's reaction; but what had he found? Not a thing you could bank on. This whole setup was like a mirage. That talk he'd been hearing. Crammed full of hidden meanings, nothing you could get your teeth firmly into but gritty as fisheggs rolled in sand.

Take that guy Anvil. Hard and loud when it suited his purpose but sly too and shifty, always slatting his eyes when a man wasn't looking, trimming his sails to each gust of the wind and never quite able to conceal the sharp claws of an interest transcending his job here as ramrod.

And Fox, a real cool one. No love lost between him and his range boss. Antagonism underlay every word they'd spoken. Yet he kept the man on, putting up with this friction when he could just as well have sent him hiking down the road.

Or couldn't he?

Rambo straddled a chair and put his arms over its back. Fox pulled out one of the slides of his desk and wedged a hip against it. He grimly dragged a match across the cloth of one pantsleg, taking the cigar from his mouth and carefully twirling the smooth end of it above the raveling flame. When the weed commenced to smolder he put it back in his mouth and tossed the match at a spittoon.

"You're no fool," he said through the swirling smoke. "Don't make the mistake of taking me for one, either. You came up here for something. It wasn't forty a month and found."

Rambo laughed. "Let's hear the rest of it." He thought Fox was a pretty smart cookie. "What do you think I came up here for?"

"You're no ordinary hand. I think you're hunting somebody." He said after a moment, "I hope to hell it's not me."

"Why do you imagine I might be interested in you?"

Fox growled impatiently. "Answering one question by asking another is a standard procedure with government dicks. I suppose they sent you here to look into Barred Circle . . . ?"

Rambo didn't help him out.

"I'm going to tell you something," the rancher said finally. "I've got my tail in a crack and I don't like the feeling."

"If any member offend you—"

Fox, staring, shook his head. "It isn't quite that simple." He said like a man cautiously feeling his way, "There's some kind of squeeze play

55

shaping up in this vicinity and by all the signs and signalsmokes I'm apt to wind up right in the gun-banging middle of it."

Rambo studied the man across a watchful reserve.

The ranchman said, turning blunt, "I'll put my cards on the table. If you're not already tied into this deal it would be worth quite a bit to bring you in on my side."

That was blunt enough in all conscience. This fellow was proving a little too shrewd for comfort. Considering him uneasily Rambo reflected there were some things a man was better off not knowing. Some types of knowledge could be construed as implication and facts, sometimes, could be very much like time bombs—one-way tickets to places no one craved to go.

"Are you trying to bribe an officer?"

Fox's eyes shone sharp as daggers now. "I said *if you weren't tied into it.* Let's quit beating about the bushes. Either you're a dick or you're not a dick—which is it?"

"You don't expect me to answer that one."

Fox grinned a little, too. "All right. The man who built Barred Circle made a hell of a lot of enemies. He's gone now, safely out of the way, and these gents he climbed over—those that are still around—have all got their knives out, figuring to get back what he took with compound interest."

56

This was dangerous ground but, thinking of Lucie Anna, Rambo said: "What part are you after?"

"Not one goddam chunk! I'm satisfied now. I don't want no government agents breathing down my neck—"

"Then keep out of it."

Fox, puffing smoke like a wood-burning locomotive, took a couple of turns around the room. Stopping in front of Rambo's chair he said abruptly, "I told you I had my tail in a crack. On top of the vulnerable position I'm in by virtue of owning the second largest outfit, my range boss is one of the fellows Deke Overpack put out of business—the most unforgiving one," he said bitterly. "He's determined to smash Barred Circle no matter what means it takes!"

"Get rid of him then. Put yourself in the clear."

"I can't," Fox said with his cheeks suddenly haggard.

"Has he got something on you?"

"Yes," Fox said with an explosive intolerance. "He's got me over a barrel. I suppose every man does one foolish thing in his lifetime. He knows something about me I can't afford to have get out."

He flung his mangled cigar into the cuspidor. "That's why I've got to have help. I can't cope with him myself. I've got to have some fellow whose word's above suspicion, someone tough as he is to watch his every move and, when all the chips are down, to tell the truth about this business."

He looked at Rambo desperately. "You know what a stake I've got here. I won't haggle over price, by God—you can write your own ticket!"

It was too late for Rambo now to say he wasn't a government agent. He had let the man's talk run too far and was trapped with the role whether he liked it or not.

One thing he *could* do, and he did that right away. He said, "I'm not here to look into that Barred Circle mess, Fox—" and knew this was no good when the man said:

"You're not?"

Something in the ragged climb of those brows, and in the obvious wonder peering out the man's eyes, warned Rambo not to stop there, and he said grudgingly, "I'm here to look into the death of a woman."

Fox appeared to consider. "That's all right. You can work on both jobs." He fetched out his silver case and got another cigar from it, smelling of the leaf while he stared back at Rambo thoughtfully. "I wasn't aware any woman had died here."

"Not here," Rambo said. "She died back in Texas while I was off on something else. I cold-trailed him here and lost the sign in these mountains."

"So you took this job with Swallowfork as

protective covering while you looked around. Why did you shoot Brick?"

All the breath Steve Rambo had hold of climbed into his throat and got wedged there.

Fox looked him over. "Did you imagine I was swallowing that hogwash of Anvil's? I never figured for a minute you were holed up at that lineshack. You've had trouble with Anvil or you wouldn't have his gun."

Rambo remembered picking it up then off the table at Barred Circle. He said, "You've damned good eyes, Fox."

The Swallowfork owner bit the end off his cigar. "I've simply learned to use them. Now suppose you tell me the straight of that business."

Rambo told of going to town, of what had happened at the stable.

Fox's cheeks turned dark, his voice was desperate. "Do you see what I mean? There is nothing too low for that fellow to put his hand to, and everything he does will be laid at my door—they'll all say I put him up to it!"

He strode about in frustrated fury. "You've got to help me! I can't stand much more of this and keep my—"

"You ever think of shooting him?"

The ranchman stared. He swung away with a bitter laugh. "He's got the whole deal down on paper. It's in the Valley Bank at Phoenix, to be opened if anything happens to him."

He tramped around the room. He said across his shoulder: "What about this skunk you're after—what kind of a looking man is he?"

"I don't know."

The rancher's head twisted around.

Rambo shrugged. "Fairly tall, I'd say—about your height. Not too heavy. Clean shaven at the outset, been described to me as handsome. Gave the name of Kramer. He was riding a blaze-faced bay in Texas."

"And you tracked him clean to the Superstitions?"

"I cold-trailed him most of the way. He had his horse replated at Sierra Blanca, had his left hind reset at Ysleta. He crossed the Rio east of Chupadera and when he got into the San Mateos I came pretty near losing him. At Horse Springs he had a *bayo coyote* and was wearing a different outfit. Sporting a mustache, too, which he no longer had when he stopped over at Alpine."

Rambo loosed a thin smile at Fox's incredulous stare. "Trailing's not too hard when a man understands what he's looking for. In the damp ground around a water hole tracks will stay reasonably sharp quite awhile. At one point I was less than ten days behind him."

"But across one state and half across two others!"

"Easier to trail a horse than it is a man afoot. When the horse is packing a rider certain

60

idiosyncracies in the way he sits his saddle generally tend to show up in the hoof tracks; and I had other things to go on. This fellow has a habit when he's nervous, tired or uncommonly irritated of rubbing the balls of his thumbs with the next two fingers. Several rannies I talked to spoke about that; and he made the mistake of keeping away from big towns."

"Where'd you lose him?"

"Just south of Post Oak. It's what I went over there last night for—I thought I'd prowl around and listen. He swapped horses again at Radium. I saw his *bayo coyote*. Packed a Gourd-and-Vine brand. It was the horse I'd been following."

Fox, shaking his head, toasted the end of his Havana over a match flame again. "He's probably well into Canada by this time."

"The fellow at the feed corral where he left that dun seemed sure he'd seen him before. Couldn't place him, but said he had the notion the man raised cattle in this country. If he does I'll find him."

Through the smoke curling round him Fox's stare looked a little queer. "What'd this woman die of?"

Rambo stared at him blankly.

"What I mean," the rancher explained, "it seems damn funny to me they'd put a U. S. Marshal—"

Rambo said bleakly, "The 'woman' was my sister. Barely seventeen."

The rancher's eyes grew wide. He pursed his lips in a soundless whistle. "Merciful Christ! No wonder you went after him!" He stood awhile deep in thought. "There don't seem to be any hell of a lot to go on but I might find out who's been away from these parts recent. I can sure do that much for you."

He went over to his desk and pulled out the middle drawer. "You fixed all right for cash?"

"I've got enough," Rambo said.

The rancher's eyes scrinched against his smoke. "You've been here about three weeks—that linecamp job's no good to you. You've got to have a reason for getting out and around. I'll try to pin down the whereabouts of everyone because it might look suspicious if you were to ask a lot of questions; but, as Swallowfork's strayman, you can ride where you please and nobody'll be the wiser. It'll help you keep tabs on that fence-crawling Anvil, too. You can report direct to me; I'll make sure that he understands that."

Rambo shook his head.

"You can name your own price," Fox said harshly, and tossed a roll of bills across to him. "There's five hundred dollars. Any more you've got coming you can have when the job's done. If Barred Circle's wrecked I want it pinned square on Anvil."

7

Rambo covered the longest part of eighteen miles before he found out what was ailing him. It wasn't reaction to telling Fox about Della or to knowing he hadn't been entirely frank with the ranchman. It wasn't even the black suspicion he'd seen clawing through the range boss when Anvil had been told about Fox making him strayman, though he yet could see in memory the wicked look the man had thrown him. The disquiet of these things still prowled the back of his mind along with what that girl had stirred, but the real trouble went deeper and came from taking Fox's money without an honest intention of earning it.

Until he'd taken that money he had owed the rancher nothing, but along with its acceptance had come an obligation as morally binding as the one he'd contracted eating grub with that girl. Telling himself such notions were preposterous neither helped to get rid of them nor enabled him to regard himself with any particular degree of comfort. Again his soul was the battleground in a recurrent clash between training and natural instinct with his better nature scorning the shoddy road he sought to travel.

Training was a rock that could not compromise

with expediency, ever and always reiterating that two wrongs never turned up a right; but Rambo rebelled with all a red-blooded man's fierce intolerance of anything so contrary to the hard-learned dictums of experience. He had taken, he knew, the only course possible without irrevocably jeopardizing the whole sum and substance of the purpose which had fetched him into this country. Barred Circle's feud had no part in this, and he was filled with an implacable hatred which could only be purged in the hot flames of vengeance.

Rambo knew what the Scriptures had to say about vengeance, but the remembrance of Della's face spurred him on through two weeks of continuous searching which took him through every ranch in the region and repeatedly into the barrooms of town, regardless of the furor and black looks he stirred up there.

Half the country had him pegged for a tinbadge now and Crooked Nose George, the town marshal of Post Oak, had asked him point-blank who the hell he was prowling for. "You'll know," Rambo said, "when I line my sights on him."

One place he had not gone to, resentful of the interest which kept him mindful of it. In streams, on sand, against the turquoise blue of continuing sunny skies her face and shape were constant challenges but he stayed away from Barred Circle. Fox, through this time, turned up nothing at all but the repeated assurance that he was still digging at it.

So was Rambo. He had not given up even though all sign had vanished. He knew the man he sought was holed up around here somewhere and he bided, always listening, grimly silent, constantly watchful. He'd talked again with that fellow at the feed corral in Radium but, while he profanely insisted he remembered the dun horse's rider, he couldn't put a name to him or recall the least clue which might point to the man's present whereabouts.

More and more of Rambo's time, these nights, was spent around Post Oak. A deterrent to business, he prowled the town now openly, contemptuous of the wooden looks, the scowls and whispers which sprang up behind him. He knew what this town thought of him. He knew the hatred he had roused in its denizens who had pasts to protect which they feared he might uncover. But even more they feared his stare and the bone-butted Colt whose weight filled out the dark scuffed holster thonged low on his right leg.

A man had tried one night to drygulch him, some cheap crook he had never laid eyes on before, at the mouth of the alley passing back of the Silver Trinket. Rambo, firing three times, had broken both the man's wrists and a kneecap. After this demonstration several others left town without bothering to have their mail forwarded, one of them the owner of a highly profitable gambling house.

And then one day he ran into Overpack again.

He was cruising through pine timber along the side of a mountain across from Needle Canyon with the sun high overhead when, without warning, he came into a clearing cluttered with old stumps and saw a weathered cabin built into the far dark line of red-barked boles.

Two grimy windows, one at either side of the near-shut door, were set like blowsy eyes below the thatch of an askew roof which, drunkenly sagging on rickety poles, gave indifferent cover to what remained of a porch. Across its wabbly railing ran a warped and cracked gray plank. On this, if a man had sufficient patience, might still be made out the ghosts of letters which had spelled RAID'S STORE.

Rambo's interest was not centered on the plank. His glance was fixed in narrowing wonder on the softly whickering hipshot horse optimistically secured to the farthest of the roof's spindling uprights. This, he was thinking, might well be Kramer's hideout.

He couldn't see the animal's brand.

A cold pulse of warning brushed like wind across his nerve ends as he thoughtfully eyed the horse and the decrepit building back of it. Thoroughly watchful, he got out of the saddle and walked to the edge of the porch and stopped. He loosened the gun in his holster, catching no sound at all from within.

The sagging boards of the porch protested his weight and the wrenched-open door skreaked as bad as a gate hinge but the place wasn't empty. There was stock on the shelves that lined the back wall and a coffee mill, of the hand-drive variety, still discernibly red beneath a dun coat of dust, was bolted to the top of a grimy old counter. And midway down the length of this counter, grounded on the pages of a spread-open newspaper, were the bare forearms of a shirt-sleeved fat man whose tan pants were held up by one frayed suspender.

"This place open for business?"

The fat man twisted his head around. His rheumy stare rummaged Steve without particular interest. Hauling it back toward his paper he remarked in a kind of choked-up whine, "You'll hev to pitch it louder, mister. I'm a mite deef this mornin'."

Rambo, regarding him dubiously, was about to take the fellow's advice when something abruptly went thumpety-bump behind a burlap-hung door-way beyond the end of the counter.

It was not very loud but Rambo's head was twisting toward it when the fat man wheezed, "You reckon a goddam shoat knows when he's bound for a fry pan?"

"Caught yourself a wild one, eh?" But even as he said it, even with the tension falling out of his bunched muscles, Rambo's grin went away and left him staring blackly. "That was a shade too slick for a man that's hard of hearing. Get back against those shelves and keep your mitts plumb empty."

The burlap swayed and a man stepped out of the back room grumbling, "What's this sport—" and stopped, seeing Rambo.

Rambo's smile loosed the gleam of hard white teeth. "You sure do get around. What did you do with your horse?"

Colorado stood as though not yet quite certain which way he wanted to play this. There was caution in his cheeks and maybe an edge of nerves showing thinly behind the gleam of his wide-open eyes, but there was no fright in evidence and not much surprise. He kept his hands in plain sight and presently smiled a little too, and he said, "Back in the timber," and then some of the buried anger got loose and the blaze on his chin showed a deeper color. "Sometime you'll get that long nose of yours burnt. Did you think you was goin' to find cows in here?"

Rambo said: "What'd you do—stub your toe back there?"

The fat man's face stayed blankly unreadable but the gun fighter's eyes were growing too sly for comfort, nor did Rambo care for the way they kept shuttling between himself and the fat man—as though they were trying to tell the guy something. Which they probably were.

A feeling of wildness got into the air and the stillness built up and got tighter and tighter. Indecision still clung to Colorado's stare but very soon it would be gone. Very shortly one of this pair was going to step outside of caution and Rambo, bleakly considering this from the bitter vulnerability of his stance midway between them, knew he had to make his choice now.

He could crowd Colorado and show his back to the fat man, or he could try backing up to the door he'd come in by, hoping hawklike to hold them with the power of his stare till he could leap outside in a dash for his saddle. This would be stretching hope one hell of a ways and probably taken by these vinegarroons as sure proof of weakness—the last thing Rambo could afford in this predicament.

He said, walking toward Colorado, "Get out of my way; I'm going to have me a look at that trussed-up shoat," and saw startled hatred explosively flare behind those pinched cheeks, behind the color of that stare. He watched sweat crack through the man's gleaming skin. With barely three strides to go, and the pressure near unbearable, a long reedy breath rushed out of Colorado. Somebody back of Rambo said:

"Just stop right there an' reach for the stars!"

· · ·

At Barred Circle Deke Overpack's daughter had called her brother three times to a belated mid-morning breakfast before, provoked past propriety, she had finally flung open the door of his room to find it empty, the covers turned back on the unslept-in bed.

She felt numb, for a moment wholly incapable of thought. Then the blood came pounding back into her head and she saw, with her glance flashing over the room, that he had not been gone the whole night. It had been late when he came in here, almost twelve, she remembered, and the two Tesuque ashtrays had been clean then, fresh emptied. Now they were both crammed with the smoked-short butts of hand-rolled quirlies. Counting them she judged he must have left just before first light—about four o'clock.

She hastened out to the corral and heard his favorite pony nicker. This was why she hadn't missed him when she'd fed the stock before fixing her breakfast. But a count of them now showed one horse short; he'd taken the cutting horse, Tony.

She'd felt a little better then, thinking he'd been inspired to make himself useful. This good feeling had lasted all the way to the bedgrounds where the crew was in the process of short-handedly assembling a trail herd. But one look at Jay's face after asking about Faron told her clearer than words her brother hadn't shown up here.

"Lord, I'm sorry," Allison said. "You want me to call the boys—"

"We can't bring the work to a standstill every time he takes it into his mind to wander off. I'll find him," she said grimly, and turned her horse toward town.

But she hadn't found him in town and no one in town would own to seeing him. She had spent three hours in the embarrassing search, not minding for herself but hounded by the fear of what he might have done this time. She even walked into Madam Farradeaux's brothel, but she didn't find Faron Overpack.

It was almost dark when she got back to the ranch. She did up the chores, hardly conscious of anything but the cold and dreadful feeling of foreboding which had hold of her. Time and again she assured herself that Faron would be all right, that he was probably lying drunk some-place and would come home when he became sufficiently sober. But, knowing the temper of Barred Circle's enemies, she was unable to put much trust in this. If only that rider who'd helped them . . .

She clenched her fists angrily, determined not to think of him. All the natural things she might have felt in that connection had died a-borning there on the porch when he had grudgingly admitted being employed by Swallowfork. No wonder he'd been so careful about withholding his name, knowing all the while how she must feel about Forko Fox.

Yet he was the kind of man she'd dreamed of in the aloneness of her solitude. Indefinably but indelibly different. A man's kind of man and yet a woman's kind, also. Not a pusher, but capable; she recalled the hard efficiency of his every move and gesture. Yet he'd quietness, a tranquillity, a deference which she, used all her life to roughness, had found enormously attractive. She liked the soft Southern drawl of the way he'd strung out even his briefest remark, the calm smile in his eyes, that clean flash of white teeth. Knowing him had somehow seemed to change everything until the coming of Allison had forced the admission that he was working for Swallowfork—prime mover behind every heartache she was faced with.

Lucie Anna was not the kind to cry over the loss of what might have been; she was too practical for that. Perhaps this man had been too new with Swallowfork to have understood what breed of polecats he'd allowed himself to team up with— but, even were this so, he had no excuse after coming into that stable. He had known then what sort of outfit paid his wages.

She went into the house, her worried thoughts back with Faron. She hung her hat on a chair back and stood a moment by the table, wholly miserable, frightened too, yet forcing herself to face the possibility that what this time had happened to Faron might have nothing to do with his fondness for whiskey. He might be lying somewhere crippled; he might be bushwhacked—even dead.

She had no illusions about Swallowfork's intent. Too much water had passed under the bridge for her to doubt Fox aimed to annex Barred Circle. He would do this if he could and if he couldn't he meant to smash it like you'd pulp a snake and pick up what was left of the pieces.

Tomorrow she'd have the crew search the range. And she would be riding with them, determined to leave no stone unturned. If they failed to find Faron then she would know—But she wouldn't let her thoughts go that far.

She was standing above the heat of the stove, with potatoes in the skillet and a cut of warmed-over steak, when she caught the sound of horses.

8

Rambo, gritting his teeth, took another pair of steps and got his left fist anchored in the gun fighter's shirtfront. One savage yank as he pivoted on a boot heel reversed their positions and swung the snarling Colorado square in front of Anvil's pistol.

The gun fighter tried to slam a knee into Rambo's groin and, failing, hurled his body leftwards, yelling, "You can get him—blast the bastard!" lifting both knees at once, his weight pulling Rambo floorward before his tangled reflex could let go of the fellow's shirt.

Anvil fired but he was in too much of a hurry and Rambo, tearing loose of the gun fighter's fingers, rolled behind the end of the counter, hearing Anvil's slugs bite into wood. He came off the floor and into a crouch, partially hidden by the shape of the coffee mill, and drove two shots whistling past the fat man as his bulk cleared the counter in a dash for the door.

Colorado, teeth bared, had a gun in his hand smashing paint off the coffee mill and, in that bedlam, ducking back of the counter Rambo bolted its length and sprang erect, Colt lifting, within three strides of the opening. The fat man, not quite through it, whirling, emptied his pistol into the canned goods and fell sprawling across the rotten boards of the porch as Rambo's gun barked answer.

Lead screamed past Rambo's cheek and he dropped spraddled out like a mallet-struck steer. Anvil let out a shout and came plunging forward. Colorado's yell set him back on his haunches. Though he was out of Rambo's sight he was still in the open and Steve was gauging the chances of coming up to pot him when the gun fighter growled:

"If the guy's cooked he's cooked, an' if he ain't we'll git him—but not by no damn stunt like that! Use what God give you! Go knock out that winder an' take a squint through the door—"

"You runnin' Swallowfork now?"

"Don't be a fool, Lew! The way to take—"

"I've already took him."

"Two will git you ten you ain't."

"All right," Anvil said, "go down the back of that counter an' we'll mighty quick find out."

Through the fading echoes and the stink of burnt powder Rambo, thumbing fresh loads into the gut of his pistol, heard the gun fighter's boots commence to work toward him. He said, "I wouldn't do it, Buster," and heard Colorado stop.

"Damn it," Anvil snarled, "you goin' to smoke him out or ain'tcha?"

"I'm pretty comfortable where I'm at."

Several seconds dragged past and Rambo did his share of guessing. Then the Swallowfork boss, hammering out a little boot sound, growled, "I'm goin' to—"

But Rambo wasn't listening. He wasn't fooled, either. He kept both eyes on the coffee mill end of the counter and, to make the possibilities appear even more inviting, he got the ramrod's confiscated hogsleg out of his chaps pocket and lefthandedly sent it skittering in the direction of the door.

It got the same reaction a scratched match would from powder. Anvil's keyed-up nerves clamped finger to trigger. Colorado, taking it hook, line and sinker, came lunging smackdab into Rambo's cocked focus. In the last split-second Rambo, soft in the head, tipped his gun down. The bullet that should have sounded taps for Colorado merely smashed his left hip and sent him reeling into the shelving under a descending shower of canned goods.

It was ludicrous rather than deadly, painful enough to Colorado no doubt but nothing to what his intention had merited. Rambo, springing up, was just in time to see Anvil's rear and his fluttering vest flaps clearing the porch in a mighty leap. He threw a slug screeching over the man's head for luck and turned back to survey the cursing half-buried gun fighter.

He removed temptation by picking up the

man's weapon and chucking it through the one still intact window. Colorado, with blood all over his pantsleg, raised a stare filled with outrage. "You fixin' to let me die here?"

"It doesn't make no never-mind to me what you do," Rambo answered and, cuffing the burlap out of his way, went into the back room to the pound of departing hoofbeats. There was a man tied onto a filthy cot there and the man was Faron Overpack. Reeking of whiskey.

But, when he got him cut loose, Rambo found something else. The boy wasn't drunk. He'd been methodically, coldbloodedly tied up and beaten insensible.

The wicked swing of Rambo's stare went from the meat hook in the ceiling to the bloodstained quirt half under the cot. He stood there woodenly a moment and then with insucked breath he brushed the burlap aside and went back to the groaning gun fighter.

"Which one of you did it?"

Colorado had his shirt off and was gloweringly tearing it into strips. He didn't look up and didn't answer and Rambo, suddenly through with patience, grabbed a fistful of hair and clouted him. "You'll talk, by God, or I'll clout it out of you!"

The gun fighter, twisting his head, glared up like a broken-backed rattler. A spate of foul language rushed through his clenched teeth but, when he saw Rambo's fist rise again, he snarled, "Anvil!"

"What for?"

"He wanted to find out somethin'."

"Go on," Rambo said, "unless you want some of what he got."

"The kid wouldn't yap. I don't guess he knowed, anyway."

"So you boys worked him over—"

"I tell you I never touched him!"

"What did Cold Jaw want to find out?"

"I dunno. He kep' askin' him about some kind of stones—"

"What kind?"

"One of 'em's got a sunburst gouged into it. Another one looks like a horse's head with the jaws open; one ear's laid back an' the other's straight up." He licked his cracked lips and his hate-filled eyes turned sullen. "Don't ask me what—"

"Where are these stones?"

Colorado's cheeks came around gray with pain but Rambo cared nothing at all about that. He had a new slant on this deal and his look was like granite when he abruptly stepped back, lifting the sixshooter out of his holster. "You ever been whipped with the barrel of a pistol?"

The gun fighter rolled the whites of his eyes. He writhed back like a sidewinder, face pulled away from his teeth in a snarl. Just the same he was cagy. "You wouldn't hit a man what couldn't hit back."

"When I think what you hardcases did to that kid I could work you over with a good deal of pleasure. Now where are those stones?"

"I dunno where they're at—on Barred Circle range, I guess. I ain't never seen 'em."

"What else did Anvil want to know?"

Colorado shook his head. "That's all he ast about. Them stones. You could fry me in lard an' I couldn't tell you no different."

"Don't tempt me," Rambo growled and, on a sudden impulse, stepped across to the door. The fat man was gone and so were both horses. He stepped out on the porch, being careful of rotten boards, and cut a glance toward the trees where they came up behind the cabin. He shoved his gun back in leather and walked into them, keeping his eyes peeled.

He found the Swallowfork horses about two hundred yards back. He tightened both cinches and led them around to the door. Leaving them on dropped reins he went back in and carried Faron out, not trying to revive him, knowing this trip would be hard enough on him anyway. He was more than a little dubious about moving him at all but he dared not leave him here.

He laid him on the ground and went back in and got a blanket. Using this to pad the brass horn of the Hamley, he lifted the unconscious Faron aboard and carefully took a few hitches with rope to make sure he stayed put with a minimum of chafing. Then, about to swing onto the other horse, he began to wonder what had happened to the mount Overpack had arrived on. There'd only been these two back in the trees, and only two out in front here when he'd gone into the shooting— his own and the tied one. He finally shrugged, thinking likely they had driven Faron's off.

He shoved his foot in the stirrup. The gun fighter's outraged yell pulled his head around.

"You fixin' to go off an' leave me in this shape?"

"It's the same shape you've had all your life, ain't it? You won't starve," Rambo said, "and you sure as sin can't ride. What do you want me to do—put a hole through your head?"

It was solid dark, with a wind romping down off the higher slopes, when Rambo got his second look at Barred Circle. The only light he could see was in the kitchen of the house and he didn't know what that black yard might hold for him. He'd been taking it pretty easy on account of the beat-up Faron; now he slowed a little more, watchful eyes raking the gloom while his ears caught up stray sounds and he wondered where the dog was. He didn't like the thought of Faron's sister being here by her lonesome. And, if she wasn't by herself, he knew there might very well be trouble, remembering how he'd quit this place that other time he'd come over here.

He pulled up and sat scowling at the house's single light. After a moment he lifted his gun from its sheath, punched out the two empties and replaced them with fresh ones. He put the gun back in leather and sat listening awhile to the waterfall sound of the wind in the cottonwoods, finally tugging the reins of the led horse and sending the one between his legs slowly forward again.

The girl had offered him a job and he was minded now to take it. He could handle Fox's chore probably better for him here than he could ever do at Swallowfork, and what this spread was up against was not being played for marbles. He thought of what Fox had told him and decided the ranchman lacked a couple of cogent facts. Considering what he'd heard and seen at Raid's Store this noon, he reckoned this deal was like to get plumb ugly before it showed any signs of getting better. One thing he was sure of: This Barred Circle was no fit place for any girl to be hanging around without gun-handy menfolks. He wouldn't put anything past Anvil now.

He rode into the yard still keeping both ears cocked. He was halfway across it, sixty feet from the porch, when the lamp in the kitchen flared once and went out. He stopped again, uneasily wondering if he'd got this figured right. It didn't *have* to be the girl who had been using that light in the kitchen. It *could* be someone Anvil had sent over here.

He dropped a hand to the butt of his pistol; and then the girl's voice called, "Stop right there and sing out if you don't want a load of buckshot."

Relief rushed through Rambo and, in the reaction of the moment, he said with perhaps more exuberance than the occasion actually warranted, "Gosh all hemlock, Lucie. Going to ask me to get down, aren't you?"

He heard the sharp catch of her breath and, suddenly smiling, was fixing to swing his leg over the cantle when her voice came again, hard and cold as a well chain. "Is your name Rambo?"

"You could just as easy call me Steve—"

"Who's that with you?"

"Faron. Where's the dog?"

"If it's Faron," she said, "why doesn't he say something?"

Rambo, assessing her tone, answered quietly, "He's not talking right now," and swung out of the saddle. "If you'll get that bed ready I'll fetch him in. Put some water on, too—put plenty of salt in it. And get some clean rags."

He knew she hadn't moved but, ignoring the gun she probably had in her hand, he went around to her brother and started undoing knots. Faron was still unconscious but groaned as

Rambo eased him out of the saddle. Steve got him over his shoulder and tramped toward the porch, wondering if perhaps he hadn't better go for a doctor.

He heard the light tap of the girl's hurried steps and a lamp's yellow flame spilled a wedge of bright gold across the porch flooring, inescapably illuminating Rambo's tall shape. He pulled open the screen and went in with his burden, the girl running ahead to make a light in the bedroom. He didn't see the shotgun but as he bent over the bed, easing the man's weight onto it, he felt a tug at his hip; when he stepped back she had his pistol pointed at him.

He said gently, "That's all right. Just be careful it don't go off."

Her lithe shape had the grace of a blooded mare, head high, nostrils flaring. Her eyes looked almost black in this light and they were wild with the outrage that whitened pinched cheeks. "What have you done to him?"

"He's just like I found him. All I've done is fetched him home."

"That's a damn puny story from the man who has managed to fool all of Post Oak—hardly worthy of your talent. You ought at least to have been able to dish up something I could swallow."

"Expect I could if I'd been trying. But that's the trouble with the truth, ma'am; sometimes it goes against all a person's experience. But the truth is what you're getting. I was traveling through this timber along a shelf above a canyon. The pines thinned out and there was this shack with a horse tied in front of it. Sign on the railing said 'Raid's Store' so I stepped in." He related the sequence and wound up with his finding of Faron.

She looked at him scornfully. "And you thought I'd believe that?"

"I see no reason why you shouldn't."

She said grimly, "Raid's Store is a relic that hasn't been used in twenty years. And the rest of it's just as impossible. Not a man in this country, except the boys on my payroll, would go out of his way to favor Barred Circle; they stand around like vultures waiting for the wolves to get done with it—the *Swallowfork* wolves," she said in the tone a man would put to a curse. "You're not fooling me, Rambo, and neither is Fox. Now go tell him I said so—go on! get moving!" She pulled back the hammer of his gun to full cock.

Rambo shook his head slowly. "You're upset and I can't blame you. You're up against something rough here, but you're wrong about me and you're wrong about Fox. You're right not to trust the most of these people but Fox is one man who's got nothing against you. He knows what Swallowfork's doing; he knows what the score is but he can't help himself. That range boss has got him backed up against a wall."

She looked at him pityingly in the silence of pure astonishment. But she kept the gun level and now a hard taunting smile ran over her lips. "You're a gullible fool or else you take me for one. Forko Fox is behind every misery I've known. He's tried for years to smash Barred Circle. When he finally got it through his head he wasn't big enough he had Deke Overpack dry-gulched. My father was no saint—I'd be the last one to say so. But what he took he took by brute force. He didn't sneak around with a knife up his coatsleeve."

"Fox doesn't strike me as that sort, either."

"Then you're blind!" She said harshly, "You asked what was wrong with our marshal—go talk to him about Forko Fox. Talk with anyone who's been in these hills a few years. Watch the rat look out of their eyes. Watch them wriggle. But don't try to feed me any pap about that ramrod—that's the craziest thing you've said to me yet. Anvil's hateful and he's vindictive but he's never been anything more than a shadow—the hell-black shadow of Forko Fox!"

There was, Rambo saw, no use in arguing with her. She had been too long exposed to the poisoned aura of this country. She believed what she'd been raised to believe, the distortions of hate and prejudiced malice which were part and parcel of the feuds her father'd fought here. You could see she was completely honest, but it was the honesty of ignorance; she simply did not know the truth. All things she saw through the eyes of Deke Overpack and nothing but time could make her realize this. Fox had been entirely right to look for crucifixion if Barred Circle crashed under Anvil's machinations. In this country Deke Overpack had obviously been hated, but a lot of this had come from strength and, now that Deke was gone, that hate was leveled at Swallowfork's owner, the natural price a man paid for vast acreage and the influence this gave him over other men's lives.

"I'd probably feel the same if I was standing in your boots," Steve nodded, "but one of these days you're going to learn how wrong—"

Her lips curled. "I'll chance that." She motioned him toward the door with his gun.

About to step through, he turned and glanced back at the shape on the bed. "Be a good idea to have a sawbones come out and take a look at your brother—"

"The depth of your concern was very adequately displayed in the way you had him tied onto that horse. Eight miles of jouncing over rocks and through brush—"

"I did the best I could—"

"The best you could to put him out of his head forever!"

Her eyes cut like a whip. The clamp of her grip around the butt of that pistol got so tight he thought she meant to kill him right there.

He was not a man greatly given to worrying, but all the way down the dim stretch of that hall his back muscles crawled in expectation of impact. His hair was damp with prickles of sweat when in the kitchen, moments later, he forced himself to turn and make one final attempt. "You offered me a job—"

Her laugh cut through his words. An ugly, dangerous sound that wasn't far removed from hysteria. The silence crept back. She smiled with her eyes bleak as malpais and the rest of her face like something dragged through a knothole. "I thought you'd be getting around to that. It's what you came back for, wasn't it? Fetching Faron home was to soften me up *but there isn't any more of that soft stuff left in me!* I'm going to shoot you just like I would a snake—"

She broke off, head twisting to the sound of hoofs. Rambo snatched the pistol and, with his eyes diamond bright, whirled and blew out the lamp.

He couldn't tell where the girl was or whether she'd got her hands on that shotgun. Quick as his glance could pierce the outside dark he saw a body of horsemen filing into the yard, their black shapes fanning out to command all the exits. Someone cleared his throat and a gruff voice said, "I don't like to be a-botherin' you, ma'am, but this here is a posse. You might as well git that lamp lit. We got our sworn duty to do an' it'll be better all around if we're allowed to do it peaceable."

9

Whatever the girl's thoughts, she could be no more astonished than Rambo was himself, for that was Crooked Nose George, the Post Oak marshal.

"What do you want?" she asked out of the stillness.

"We got a warrant for your brother."

She'd be thinking, Rambo guessed, about that business of Injun Charley's girl, that ugliness Anvil had staged at the stable.

"A warrant for Faron?"

"That's right, ma'am. Suppose you git that lamp lit now an' ask him to kindly step out here. No cause for any heroics. If he ain't done what he's accused of he'll be let go as soon as he proves it."

"And what if I tell you he isn't here?"

"Wouldn't be no use in your lyin', ma'am. We didn't make this ride to git waved around thataway. Just tell him to step out. It could git a mite onpleasant if we was to hev to come in there after him."

"But I tell you—"

"Better not, ma'am. Hughie, strike a light an' take a look at them hosses."

Leather skreaked. A man swung down with a jingle of spur sound. The flame of a flaring match raveled over the mounts Steve and Faron had come in on. The stick burned short and the man dropped it, saying, "Swallowfork, George, an' still pretty ropey."

"Guess that cinches it. Hadn't no chance to git back to his own. Took what was handiest an' yanked that spare along. Which accounts for him bein' able to git here ahead of us."

In the black of sooty shadows Rambo, still watching the yard, reached a hand out, feeling for her, thinking tangible knowledge of his presence might reassure her. What he touched was firm and yielding. "He's been hurt—" She gasped, and knocked the hand away from her.

"I ain't surprised," George answered. "Some of the boys got to throwin' their lead a little wild-like when they seen this coyote comin' out the bank door after bashin' old Rammickey's head in. If he could git this far I reckon he's fit to ride back. Come he ain't, we're campin' right here till he is."

There was cold fright creeping through Lucie's voice when she said, "You're accusing him of holding up the Post Oak bank?"

"That, an' killin' Rammickey."

"But you're not a county officer! You've no jurisdic—"

"The point is, ma'am, I'm here. An' so is your

brother. We're takin' him in. I'll count so far as ten an' if he ain't stepped out—"

"Don't be in no hurry to push on the reins, George. Buckshot," Rambo said quietly, "will kick quite a hole through that posse."

At about this time Forko Fox, more bothered than he'd have cared to admit, was reining a weary horse into the ramshackle remains of what had once been a noisy place. Thief River was the handle folks had given it in its heyday, partly because of the drinkless trickle that sluggishly crept between high sandstone walls pocked with the holes of vanished treasure hunters. The camp still nourished a few crusty hardshells but its appeal, these days, was to a different class of customer, a soft-handed breed who had the facetious habit of describing the place as a "health resort."

Fox, chewing the end of an unlit cigar, eyed its scabrous buildings with a look of contempt. Not even the light of a rising moon was able to cover their shrunken bones with the glamour which legend had so generously once ascribed to them. These creaking ghosts scraped like filed tin across the rancher's sensibilities, for his was not a nature anxious to tolerate ghosts in any guise.

He saw a number of hipshot ponies forlornly hunched before the barnlike wreck of what had been the celebrated Bella Union Bar. Lamplight splashed across its twisted porch where Black Jack Ketchum had sometimes lounged banging away at bottles between the forays which had finally jerked the head off his shoulders. And there was a dim murmur of voices drifting out of the glassless windows.

The ranchman kneed his horse over alongside those others and got down, dropping his reins across the toothmarked hitch rail. "Hello," he called, at the edge of the porch, and the voice sounds stopped as though cut off with a cleaver. A chair scraped back and booted feet, coming toward him, set up a hollow clamor. A man's broad shape pulled into the open doorway, black against lampshine, and after a hostile interval a single word fell explosively out of it.

Fox said, "Gellerman?"

The odor of distrust was an overpowering rankness mingling with the smell of damp earth coming off the river but the man, abruptly turning, went shambling out of sight.

Fox remained by the tie rail, bitterly hating every part of this but knowing deep inside him he had precious little choice. A one-string bow wouldn't last much longer than a June frost in Texas in the things he saw building for the days ahead. It was like to be hell with the hide off and none but a dimwit would let dislike cloud his judgment or permit the possible cost to stand in the way of barricading his interests.

He contained himself with what patience he was able and cooled his heels in the freshening breeze until the drag of spurred boots started doorward again. Then he stepped out plain in the moonglow where there'd be no doubt both his hands were empty.

He watched the lank shape of this new man across the porch and come to a spread-legged stance a short horse-length away. The man was so thin he would have had to stand twice to cast a real shadow. He had a black-jowled face and gangling arms and his legs, with the baggy pants breeze-whipped against them, didn't look much thicker than a pair of burnt match sticks. Fox, eyeing the yellow boots, found it hard to realize he was staring at a man sought by the law of sixteen counties.

"Aren't you Forko Fox?" the man said gruffly, and there was a bright curiosity in the cant of his stare.

The ranchman nodded.

The thin man said, "I'm Gellerman."

He didn't greatly favor Fox's conception of a killer. He appeared to be clean shaven. There was a cool, probing intelligence looking out of the reticent eyes and an air of easy assurance more disturbing than open belligerence. But Fox knew his rep and, though he couldn't glimpse the nicks filed into that bonehandled gun butt, was reassured by the comfort of rumor. Twelve notches. And no colors counted but white.

There was a blur of salt cedars off there beyond the horses and, noticing these now, Fox believed he saw the key to this bravo's display of nonchalance. Doubtless he was covered by half a dozen rifles.

"It's a long ride back."

"Yes." Fox nodded. "I came over here on business." But, in the face of this fellow's disconcerting composure, he found it hard to concentrate, harder to get down to cases. The man should be nervous, uneasy and edgy; the shoe, and it was a tight one, seemed to be on the wrong foot.

The thin man said, "Did you wish to consult me in my official capacity?"

"Official . . . ?"

Gellerman laughed. "I'm the Mayor of Thief River." And then he said, suddenly bleak, "You're not interested in my plans for civic improvements. Let's get down to brass tacks. Who do you want planted and how much is there in it?"

"I'm a long way from sure I want anyone killed—"

Gellerman grinned skeptically. "Then why ask for me? If there'd been nothing on your mind more strenuous than rustling any one of these boys would have been able to take care of you.

If it wasn't something beyond the nose of the law you couldn't have been dragged within gunshot of this place. Rumor cuts both ways. You don't have to wear a mask with me."

A shadow crossed Fox's face like doubt. He stood silent a moment, then shrugged and said stiffly, "I have no intention of wearing a mask. When I go out to hire help I hire the best I can get. I've got a man I can't trust and he's quick with a gun. That's why I came over here. I want to hire you to watch him. The job's worth a grand."

"Pretty high-powered man. You got the dough with you?"

"Certainly I've got it."

"What's to keep me from taking it and dumping you in the river?"

Fox's mouth tightened up. "I wasn't born yesterday. There might be a lot more than a thousand bucks in this—"

"There had better be," Gellerman said. "I ain't risking a scalp with three thousand on it to pick up one." He smiled again, thinly. "Let's hear the rest of it."

"If you handle this right there may be other jobs. If, while guarding my interests, you should have to kill anyone, you'll get two thousand more. If trouble develops between my spread and Barred Circle there's a very good chance you may clean up considerable." He watched Gellerman carefully. "There's a place in this country for a man of real talent."

Gellerman chuckled. "I guess we talk the same language."

"You'll have to keep my name out of it."

"I took that for granted. Who's this fellow you want watched and where'll I get onto him?"

Fox still didn't like it but he dropped his voice and spoke steadily for two minutes, well knowing the risk he ran employing an outlawed man of this caliber. He was careful to make his desires specific, allowing room for unexpected developments yet guarding against loose ends which might later, through this hired trigger's greed or another's discovery, turn up to confound him.

When Gellerman nodded his understanding the ranchman passed him a packet of banknotes and climbed back into his saddle. He felt almost unclean for having to deal with such a man.

Rambo knew as soon as he spoke that he might better have kept out of this. It had nothing whatever to do with the purpose which had brought him into this country—nor had the girl. But he also knew that he could not stand by and leave her to the fears—and very possibly the dangers—she was faced with through this marshal and her relationship to Faron. He knew instinctively she'd fight for Faron with no concern for the right or the wrong of it; everything she did was in that forthright headlong fashion and, while he could acclaim the spirit that enabled her, in himself such a thing must be accounted sheerest folly. He had spoken without thinking and he was furious to realize that was what this girl could do to him.

But, regardless of the reason, he had spoken; and that gentle reminder of the efficacy of buckshot had turned that group in the yard so still the gusty wind rocking through the tops of the cottonwoods assumed the major sounds of a full-throated avalanche.

He could catch the worried twisting of heads as looks were swapped, and guessed this bunch wasn't near as anxious to back the marshal's hand as it had been. He was reminded of an old Spanish truism, that when danger strides in at the door civic consciousness and duty tend to jump for the nearest window.

But the hard facts were that nobody had jumped yet. They were still in the "tending" stage and before they could get their legs gathered under them George adroitly gave them something else to think about.

"I expect," he said with a tolerant chuckle, "you boys'll be fixin' to kick the lid off tomorrer. Unless my ears has deceived me, that was Rambo loosenin' the phlegm in his windpipe. With the hundred bucks already put up on him plus the large reward the bank is sure to pay for Rammickey's killer—"

"I can't see why anyone would offer a hundred dollars for me. I think," Rambo said, "you're trying to gull those boys, George."

"Brick," the marshal said, "had a lot of friends in this country."

Rambo, suddenly cold, demanded: "You saying I killed Brick?"

"I got a warrant here that says so."

"You might's well tear it up then. Brick was shot by the Swallowfork ramrod."

"He said you'd probably try to lay it onto him—"

"You needn't take my word for it. Ask Colorado. He was there. He saw the whole thing—in fact, he shot at Brick himself."

"Lyin' ain't goin' to help you, Rambo. Now put down that greener an' step out here peaceable an' I'll do the best I humanly can for you."

"I guess not," Rambo said. "But I'll tell you what I will do. If you'll gather up that bunch of misguided fools and get them turned around and headed off this property pronto, I'll do what I can to keep this sawed-off from splattering the bunch of you hell west and crooked."

"You defyin' the law?"

Rambo spoke with a show of contempt. "Since when was an off-bounds town constable's authority anything to worry a deputy U. S. Marshal?

I'm going to count up to seven, George. You'd better get moving."

He was almighty glad that in these deep-piled shadows George's bunch was unable to observe that all he had in his hands was the blued steel of a sixshooter housing five cartridges.

Their indecision was plain, advertised in the way their heads were twisting and turning. He was just beginning to hope his bluff might manage to stick when a gout of orange flame tore away from the hip of one of those now milling riders. Glass fell out of a nearby window and a shotgun's roar ripped the night into dollrags.

Shouts, anguished cries and the wild scream of horses welled out of the dinning echoes of that blast. And the face of the moon, peering over the barn, turned the yard bright as day, disclosing a pandemonium the like of which Rambo hoped never again to look on.

Horses were tearing around like mad, sunfishing, pitching, yet cannily avoiding the clutching hands stretched out to catch them. The shapes of three riders writhed and twisted on the ground and men fortunate enough to still be in their saddles were spurring like crazy, not caring where they went just so it got them clear of that greener. The shotgun roared again and there were no more yells or twisting, just dark blotches in the moonlight and, far off, the dim treble of fast-departing hoof sound.

10

Rambo found the lamp and fumbled the chimney off and got the wick ignited and reseated the glass tube firmly in the clasp of its tiny brass brackets. The skin at the back of his neck still prickled and inside his head that remembered clamor sank cold corkscrew tentacles into his stomach. He could stand it, he guessed, and all the nauseous details, but he sure as hell hated having to meet Lucie's eyes.

She couldn't have done it if he'd kept his mouth shut and stayed out of this. All the remembered cant from Scripture righteously flayed him for having inspired such slaughter, but the wayward side of him shrugged this away. He was sorry for Lucie's part in it but he wasn't going to be sorry for what had happened to those possemen. Reward hungry bastards! They had gotten what they'd asked for, coming rampaging out here to bully a woman and frame a poor fool who couldn't possibly have done this thing they had him charged with no matter how many stood ready to claim they'd seen him.

What Steve really hated—aside from the burden of guilt this sequence had shoved onto Lucie—was his own stupidity in not sensing sooner her brother could have been cleared if they had let that bunch have a look at him. The man't physical condition had been the key to his innocence and Rambo's bluff had thrown it away.

He lifted self-accusing eyes and stared, transfixed with open-mouthed astonishment, at the man who now stepped away from the window, at the man who now, with a bitter smile, set the shotgun carefully down against the wall. His battered face looked like a gargoyle hacked from knotty pine, but it was Faron's; and Faron's voice that said, feigning toughness, "That'll keep 'em off awhile, I guess."

Rambo scrubbed a fist across the side of his cheek; jammed mind trying to assimilate the significance of Faron's presence, of Faron's shaking hand setting down that smoking greener.

The girl was staring, too, her face bone white with strain and shock; and, suddenly, her knees were buckling and Rambo was catching her, holding her against him, mumbling things he didn't even himself understand the meaning of. "Lay her down on the floor," Faron said, "and she'll come out of it. Where's my father?"

Rambo let her down with that extreme kind of care a big man's strength generally brings to the handling of something fragile. He smoothed the skirt about her legs and stood up, looking baffled and foolish. Faron, dropping a hip to a corner of the table, said, "Just a touch of the vapors—she'll be all right. Who are you and where's Deke? Where's the rest of the outfit?"

That last part got through and Rambo pulled his glance off the girl's face and looked at Faron. He stared a long while, rubbed his cheek with his fist again, and finally said, "I'm a friend of the family. Your crew's out on the range and your father . . . maybe I'd better let Lucie handle that part."

"Something's happened to him, has it?" Faron dug the makings from a pocket of his shirt, apparently unaware the blood-stained back of it was dangling from his shoulders in stiffened shreds. "I've always figured something would. By God, I feel like I been dragged through a knothole! I've got a taste in my mouth—"

"You've had a pretty rough time. You remember going to Raid's Store?"

Young Overpack shook his head, looked kind of funny and put a hand up carefully to the white hair over his temple. He fingered it gingerly a moment; then, bringing it down, got out his papers. That was when he saw his rope-chafed wrists. He lifted puzzled eyes and stared a while at Rambo's face. "What the hell's been going on?"

"What's the last thing you remember?"

"Climbing onto that damn sunfishin' roan." He finished building his smoke, licked the end of his tongue across the flap of the paper, put the makings away and then, scowling, said, "Did he pile me again?"

"I reckon," Rambo nodded. "You got kicked in the head."

"Have I been out all this time? It was right after lunch—"

"That was five years ago."

Faron stared at him, silent. Lucie groaned, her lids fluttered and she came up on an elbow. Rambo helped her to a chair. She sat there palely for a moment and then, pulling herself together, she managed a wan smile and put her hand out to Rambo. He took her cold fingers in one big fist and rubbed them. She looked at Faron then and smiled with the tears rolling down her cheeks. She sprang up and went over to him, cupping his bruised face in both her hands, then squeezing it against her.

"Aw, Sis—" Faron growled, and pulled away from her, embarrassed.

"I think," Rambo said, "we'd better bring Faron up to date and decide what to do about this mess we've got into—that is," he said, watching her, "if you're willing to let me stay around long enough to be of some use."

Lucie, blushing prettily, dried her eyes with a quiet dignity. She was almost a different person now that her brother seemed miraculously to have recovered the use of his faculties. Evidently the treatment he had got at Raid's Store had been just what he needed to knock the kink from his mind. She said, "I guess I rather jumped to conclusions. I still can't see though," she added honestly, "why you persisted in working for Swallowfork—"

"That's a long story," Rambo said, "and it will keep. Right now you had better get to work on his back while I tell him what happened over there at that shack."

She got the water and the cloths and went to work, Faron occasionally groaning as the salty solution bit into torn flesh. Rambo repeated the story he'd told Lucie. "But why?" Faron said when he'd finished. "Why would they do a thing like that?"

"They're after this ranch," his sister told him. "They're determined to grab it or smash it if they can't. Forko Fox is—"

"Not Fox," Rambo said. "Anvil is the one."

Lucie Anna looked as though she were minded to contest that but, with a thoughtful smile, she merely said, "Swallowfork, anyway. Whoever is behind this attempt to wreck Barred Circle has all the influence and fire power of Swallowfork to work with."

"He hasn't been using me," Rambo said.

"Then it's because he hasn't needed you. Oh, it *could* be Anvil," she admitted, "but some- way I can't picture him as having that much savvy."

"When did this feud get started?" Rambo asked.

"As long as I can remember there's been trouble. When I was a little girl I used to wake up in the night to the sound of pistol and rifle fire. Time and again Deke said in my hearing it was Fox who was back of all the hell going on. He said—and Faron will bear me out in this—that it was Fox who turned all our neighbors against us. They were too scared of Deke to do very much. It took Fox quite a while to understand that. First he tried to throw the riffraff against us. Then he tried to band the small boys into a confederation, but when things started to get rough they ran out on him. The bigger spreads distrusted him too much to mix into it. That was when he began to build up this tough crew."

"Hasn't it ever occurred to you," Rambo asked, "that these things your father attributed to Swallowfork could have been, from their side of it, the mechanics of defense?"

Faron said seriously, "He might be right about that, Sis."

"I try to be fair," Lucie said, "but I can't see—"

"Let's put it this way. Did you ever with your own eyes discover Fox himself in this? Did you ever hear that he was actually directly concerned in these happenings?"

"No," said Lucie honestly; "but then he's much too shrewd, much too much of a fox to be caught in anything openly."

Rambo sighed, but then he pulled up his chin with a rueful smile. "I reckon we've whittled that far as we can," he said shrugging. "We'd better put our heads to figuring what they'll try next, now that we've run off George's posse."

"You've done enough," the girl said. "I think you had better ride over some hills—"

"You still doubting me?"

She dropped her glance for a moment and Faron, watching them, got up and went off, saying something about the need of digging out a clean shirt.

Lucie lifted her eyes. They were direct now, more personal. She was, Rambo thought, a contradictory young woman; and a very desirable one, he added grudgingly. She said, "I do appreciate what you've done for us . . . But it isn't fair, Steve, that you should get yourself involved—"

"I'm already involved—"

"Yes, but George wouldn't have—"

"George," Rambo said, "is pretty obviously part and parcel of whatever's in the wind between Swallowfork and Barred Circle. This fellow, Brick, was killed three weeks ago—"

"Right after you got Faron out of that stable. But it wasn't," she said shrewdly, "until you walked into Raid's Store that the marshal was told to pin that on you."

Rambo's smile turned a little thin but he said,

"You can't have your cake and eat it, too. You can't stretch the time element like you would a piece of rubber. You can assume Anvil carried that straight to Fox. But you can't show Fox, after Anvil's arrival, rigging up that bank deal, getting it pulled and then sending George out here to pick up Faron—"

"George had warrants for both of you!"

"George *said* he had. Look at it this way a moment. I didn't see your brother's horse when I was out to Raid's Store. There might just possibly have been enough time for Anvil, riding *two* horses, to have got to town, rigged and pulled that bank job, fixed up the warrants and—figuring I'd be here—put that posse on your doorstep."

"I don't believe it," Lucie said.

"Then how can you tie Fox into it?"

"I don't know," she admitted, "but I'm sure he is."

"What's become of your dog?"

"Someone poisoned him last night."

Faron came out of the hall with clean clothes on. "What are we going to do about these charges?"

"I don't think," Rambo said, "they'll be pushing them very hard."

"Are you really a federal marshal?" Lucie asked, and Rambo shook his head.

"But they don't know that."

"Maybe," Faron said, "that's what they've

been digging into. Waiting for proof before they slugged Brick's killing at you."

Steve had brought them up to date about that, but neither he nor Lucie had told Faron about what had happened in that Post Oak stable. Rambo said, "Did anyone come here after you last night?"

Faron scowled in obvious thought, but finally shook his head, looking baffled. "I don't know how I got over to Raid's Store."

"Do you remember them hoisting you onto that hook?"

"I don't recall a damn thing after being thrown off that roan until I picked up that greener and stepped to the window. Five years! It doesn't seem possible . . ."

"Did either of you," Rambo said, "ever come across a rock with a sunburst gouged into it? Or one that looks like a horse's head with the jaws open?"

They regarded him blankly.

"Probably hogwash," he said, and told Faron: "That's what Colorado gave as Anvil's excuse for working you over. He said Anvil kept asking—"

"Good lord!" Lucie cried. "The Peralta Mines!"

Rambo leaned abruptly forward, unaccountably excited by the connotations of her tone. "What's that?"

"The lost Peralta gold mines!" She laughed a little breathlessly. "I remember now. Deke used to talk of them—said half the fools in Arizona were off through the mountains trying to find a stone head."

"And these Peraltas . . . ?"

"They were Spaniards, several brothers, who came up out of Mexico in the eighteen forties hunting for gold in the Superstitions," Lucie said. "They're supposed to have found several mines—ten, I think—but the Indians drove them away, covering and disguising the entrance of the shafts.

"In the seventies, however, a pair of men with a map came up into this region and started prowling the hills. The way Deke used to tell it, these Mexicans—one of them was said to have been the last of the Peraltas—reopened one of the mines but were set upon and killed. One died where he fell but the other got away, later dying at Andy Starr's place on the desert, leaving Starr the map they'd used in relocating the mine they had opened.

"Meanwhile the killers, Jake Walz and Jake Wiser, fell out over the gold. Walz shot Wiser but, while Walz was hurrying back to their camp to destroy everything which would tie him to this murder, Wiser managed to reach Walker's ranch, near Florence, where he did a lot of raving. No one around here, according to Deke, gave this disjointed babbling any great amount of notice; they'd been brought up on stories of lost and buried gold mines and passed them straight through from one ear to the other."

Rambo rubbed his cheek. "What happened to the Dutchman—the one who shot his partner?"

"He turned up in Florence with a sack of jewelry rock, rose quartz that was two-thirds gold, bragging he had found an old Spanish mine. But people began asking what had happened to Wiser, and Walz high-tailed it. He was next seen in Phoenix, spending another sack of ore and still bragging of his bonanza. Hundreds of people tried to trail him but Walz was too slick. He came back a few months later with a burroload which he sold to Goldman & Company. The assay on this ran better than $10,000 a ton. This went on for several years until Walz finally, afraid for his life, came out of the mountains and stayed out. He bought some land in Phoenix and was there when the earthquake of eighty-seven shook the stuffing out of this country."

"And changed all the landmarks?"

She shrugged. "It must have changed some of them. Wiser made a map for the Walkers. Walz made a map for Julia Thomas. These maps are still bringing a few hunters into the mountains but no one, apparently, is getting anyplace. The Lost Dutchman's still lost and, as Deke was fond of saying, it will probably stay lost 'until the last trump is sounded.' "

"Just the same," Rambo said, "this could be

what's back of your troubles. Anvil's probably got some reason for thinking these stones are a clue to Walz's bonanza; and he evidently believes they're on your range—"

He broke off, staring, as a blankness dawned and spread like fright across Faron's bruised, suddenly tautened features. "They are," he croaked, and he shook as with a chill. "I was with Deke when he found them . . . the horse with its jaws open, one ear laid back and the other straight up. We had just come off the soldiers' trail . . ."

His eyes were like coals in the blue-gray pallor of his frozen face. He shook again, groaning. "That's—that's all I can remember."

11

Rambo, riding some two hours later on the shortest line between Barred Circle and Swallow-fork, was up to his ears in some dark thinking. It was clear enough now what Anvil was after. A bonanza assaying ten thousand dollars to the ton was enough to account for a lot of rough stuff and, by this token, what had happened already was less than nothing to the violence which might at any moment now descend across this range.

Somehow Anvil, or men in Anvil's pay, had got onto Deke's discovery and found out young Faron had shared it. This put a different complexion on Lucie's problems, and on the rout of George's posse—not to mention that Post Oak bank deal. But why had Faron lied? And how much had Fox's ramrod uncovered concerning Steve Rambo's past?

No one had to tell Steve he was walking on eggs. The least misstep might very well prove fatal, not only to his own reason for being in this country but to Barred Circle's future and the situation of Faron's sister.

He wasn't prepared to waste much thought on young Overpack, feeling as most did in the West of that day that any man worth his salt would fend for himself. A poor fool out of his head was one thing; a fool in his right mind was something else.

While he'd been readying himself for the ministry Rambo had tried to think like a preacher, but when he'd chucked that over he'd figured to have enough woes of his own without shouldering those of the universe. Lucie was a girl—which made her case different; but the most of his time, he told himself grimly, he owed to finding and punishing a man who counted women fit prey, that two-legged skunk who'd used the name of Deuce Kramer. It was doggone odd how that varmint had disappeared.

Steve had spent a deal of time looking around to locate someone who, when upset or deeply thinking, unconsciously rubbed his thumbs with the next two fingers. He'd found one man nursing the habit in Post Oak, the assayer, who could not by any stretch of Steve's imagination be the man he was on the prowl for. French, the assayer, was a short slob of a man, fatter even than the rubicund Wimpy who'd pretended to keep store at that shack in the timber.

Remembrance of Wimpy swung Rambo's thoughts back to Anvil. How had they gotten Faron out there? Had they picked him up at Barred Circle? Was this why Rover had been poisoned the night before? It could have been that way. Whiskey could have lured Faron out of the house; the rest would have been like taking candy from a kid. But why put stock in that tumbledown store?

He realized, with his mind harking back to it, they hadn't; he remembered the dust crust on the coffee mill, the meager stock on the dingy shelves, the faded labels on the canned goods. But why had they used the place at all? Mere chance?

Steve didn't think so. The brain back of this wasn't the kind to leave things dangling . . . Struck with that, he wondered if Lucie's conviction was so far off line as he'd been inclined to think. Granting her to be mirroring the projected thoughts of her father, could Deke, who had known both Fox and his foreman over a period of years, have been so hipped on Fox he could have overlooked Anvil? Have mistaken the devilment of one for the other?

It didn't look too reasonable. Nevertheless Steve felt reluctant to believe himself in error. He'd been trained to judge men, both in his schooling and by experience; he'd been wrong a few times, too, he recalled. But he couldn't feel he was wrong about Fox. Anvil looked much more the part, a sly, vindictive, unscrupulous scoundrel, well coached for the role of master villain. Fox was open, frank, plainly worried; there was nothing sinister about the man. The things Lucie had said were based on prejudiced conjecture and rumor; Rambo had had much experience with rumor while packing the five-pointed star at Golden—while handling that jerkline freight string, too. He knew how rumors got started, was aware how little truth they were built on. The have-nots always distrusted the haves.

His mind went back to Raid's Store.

That shack wasn't on Barred Circle. It wasn't far from it though—less than half a mile from the nearest Overpack linecamp, also abandoned in these short-handed times. If Anvil was rustling Barred Circle cattle he could be using Raid's Store as a base of supplies, or of observation; that could be Wimpy's job, a paid spy for Anvil's cow stealers. He must remember to question Lucie about their losses.

But why take Faron there? Merely to keep him out of the way while that bank job was being rigged? Perhaps, Rambo admitted, but George in that case wouldn't have looked for Faron at home without Anvil or Wimpy had ridden directly for town after quitting Raid's Store.

The most likely solution Rambo could hit on pictured Colorado fetching Faron there from Barred Circle so that Anvil could question him, free of interruption, about the stone horse head and that rock with the sunburst. Perhaps the place was near them, or Anvil had reason to suspect that it was. When Faron had balked, or in truth had not remembered, Anvil in a fury had taken that quirt to him. Warned of Rambo's approach by the fat man, Anvil had hidden behind the cabin waiting for him to go away. Faron had made a racket, forcing Colorado to create a diversion. While Rambo had been occupied with Colorado and the fat man, Anvil had slipped around and come into the store behind him, Rambo moving too fast for him to do as he'd intended. Then, when Rambo had dropped the gun fighter, Anvil in a lather of fear and fury had bolted, the fat man following suit. That slug Steve had thrown at Wimpy had apparently missed him clean.

Anvil, perhaps bent on fixing up an alibi, had probably grabbed both horses and hellity larruped for town. By the time he'd got there he'd hatched up this scheme for getting Faron off his hands and, by the same adroit move, getting in another body blow at groggy Barred Circle. He'd had the bank stuck up and Rammickey—who may have seen through it—killed. Then he'd gone to the marshal, identified the killer as Faron Overpack, and sent him thundering toward Barred Circle with that posse.

This, Rambo reckoned, was the truth of the matter. Anvil had obviously intended to get Faron killed; he could look for Barred Circle to put up some kind of fight and, in the attendant tumult, somebody with that posse would have been primed to put a slug through the fellow. The shotgun, of course, had broken that up. But what about the warrant George claimed to have for Rambo?

He hadn't much acted as though he'd looked to find Steve out there. True, Anvil had no reason to suppose Rambo would tarry after getting Faron home. When Steve had first gone to work for the Swallowfork the ramrod had taken quite a shine to Steve's bay gelding and had asked how much it would cost a man to own him. "I wouldn't price Samanthy," Rambo had said gruffly. "That horse is a pegger. You could get my right arm cheaper than him." Anvil would have laid his plans accordingly, counting that horse sure lure for an ambush. The warrant could have been fixed up earlier—if there was one.

Rambo lifted his bronc to a faster pace. Samanthy would keep. Right now Forko Fox was the gent Steve ached to see. After talking with Fox he'd probably have a better slant on this whole feuding setup. He still couldn't figure what had made Faron lie—fright, of course; but fright of whom? Rambo knew just as certain as he knew his own name young Overpack had remembered considerably more than he'd admitted.

It was hardly more than a short half hour to cook's call when Rambo walked his sweating pony into Swallowfork's silent yard. The moon's pale disk was too far down to throw much light and the bunkhouse across the way was just another black shape among the eucalyptus shadows. He knew that Anvil might have gotten home by now and, not wanting any argument, put his horse around to the back, trying to figure which window would be the one to Fox's bedroom.

He dropped off the Swallowfork bronc and was working his saddle-cramped legs creakingly nearer when the gleam of a lamp threw its shine through the cookshack. Dirty Shirt stepped hawking to the door and vigorously spat. The bronc Steve had just got off of opened its mouth in a noisy whicker. The cook's head twisted around. Scowling disgustedly, Rambo gave up caution and banged his fist several times on Fox's door.

"Who's there?"

"Rambo," Steve said; and, after a few moments, a lamp emphasized the outer darkness and Fox, knuckling his eyes, came to the door and let him in.

"Couldn't this have waited till after breakfast?"

Rambo gave him the gist of what had happened at Raid's Store and the sleep disappeared from Fox's eyes in a hurry. His hair was tousled and he'd pulled on his boots, hastily throwing a lounging robe over his pyjamas, but he didn't look ludicrous; to Rambo he looked like a badly worried man as he rubbed a whiskery jaw and said, "I don't know what to tell you. All that stuff about stones—"

"Do you suppose there's buried gold on that place? You reckon that could be what he's after?"

Fox said irritably, "It looks as though he thinks there is. Hell, there's supposed to be gold all through these mountains. Buried mines are a dollar a dozen if you can believe all the talk you can hear in this country. About thirty years ago a Dutchman named Walz was showing around a lot of highgrade rock; I never heard of Overpack showing any though."

"You ever heard about those stones?"

"Not anything that looked like a horse head. One of the clues to the Lost Dutchman—the Spanish mine Walz was supposed to have uncovered—is said to be a stone face. That's how it's described on the maps, I understand. I've never met anyone who claims to have seen it. Did you take young Overpack home?"

Rambo, nodding, told him about George's posse and the stick-up of the Post Oak bank. Reciting how the greener had broken up George's play, he wound the story up with finding the shotgun in Faron's hands.

The ranchman shook his head. "This is a fine mess now! By God, I'm glad I hired you!"

"Do you think George will push that charge?"

"I'm afraid he will," Fox said, scowling.

"But I could show the kid couldn't have been

anywhere near Post Oak and, if we can keep him clear of Anvil, Colorado will back me up."

"Colorado's dead," Fox said after a moment. "Some Indian hauled him in here just after supper last night. You can see what they'll do now; Anvil will say you murdered him and that fat man will back him up. They'll have a warrant out for you—"

"They've got one now," Steve said, and told him about Brick.

Fox took a turn about the room. He picked the butt of a cigar out of an ashtray and lit it, exhaling several lungfuls of smoke, then saying with a hard satisfaction, "Of course, if it ever comes to trial, being a marshal you've got nothing to worry about. They don't know that, they think you're bluffing; but you sure as hell can't bunk here no longer."

He rolled the smoldering weed across his teeth. "You can see that, can't you? Too risky for me to keep you here or have you openly on the books after this. Too dangerous, anyway; that sonofagun would be having you bushwhacked. The girl ought to be enough beholden to you now that you could—"

"What did Colorado die of?"

A gusty breath fell out of the ranchman. He said, on the heels of an odd, searching scrutiny, "He got kicked in the teeth with a piece of galena."

Rambo's eyes raked his face. He didn't care for that tone. It was almost as though Fox was wondering if he'd done it. But, before he had time to put the question direct, Fox said with an assumption of his former crisp authority, "Best thing you can do is get a job with Barred Circle. That way you'll be right on the ground. If that kid stuck up the bank—"

"How could he," Rambo asked, "when he was getting the tar whaled out of him at that shack above Needle Canyon?"

"How could he get out of bed and use that sawed-off on the marshal's posse?" Fox said with a sigh, "I'm not claiming he pulled that bank job; I'm just saying if he did it was probably because that outfit's about reached the end of its string. If there's anything at all we can do to pull them through I think it's up to us to do the best that we are able. Lucie's too fine a girl—"

"Can't you steer George off them?"

Fox stared at him, looking puzzled. After a moment he said thoughtfully, "When Anvil owned the west half of Barred Circle, George was his foreman. Does that answer your question?"

Outside there was a clatter like hell emigrating on cartwheels, and the cook's strident voice yelled: "Mexkin strawberries—come an' git 'em!"

Rambo frowned. "It's you that people think has got the forked stick on this country."

"Naturally," Fox smiled thinly. But then his face turned darkly sober. "I told you before I'm the obvious goat. That fellow's smarter than you think. This wasn't hatched overnight. He's got this whole region fooled—the perfect bully-puss ramrod of a grasping range hog. I know what they say; I know what they think, too. But I ain't running—I won't give him that satisfaction!"

He smashed one fist into the palm of the other. "By God, I'm not the kind that quits! Black-mail has taken that gentleman quite a ways but a man can only be pushed so far—remember that, Rambo." Some of the wildness leached out of his cheeks. "You know the truth. You know what I'm up against. The minute he smashes Barred Circle I've got him. I'll get a company of dragoons into this section and put him away for the rest of his natural!"

Rambo said, "But that girl—" and stopped with his eyes brightly narrow. Fox had turned with his head held stiffly as a man sometimes will when he's trying to hear something. Coming out of that stance he hurried over to the window and, being mindful of his shadow, peered into the yard around the edge of the drawn shade.

For a moment he stared unmoving. He said through stiff lips, "He's coming now. You better drift."

Rambo, gripped in the lift of his temper, was minded to have it out with the ramrod. The tug of this desire must have written its urge across the look of his face because the ranchman snarled, "Go on—get moving! Do you think I want any more trouble between you? Don't forget what that skunk's holding over my head—or what'll happen if he's killed! Get going!"

Rambo was eight miles from Swallowfork, better than halfway across the humps that climbed this range to Barred Circle, when Samanthy sneaked into his thoughts and swung him eastward. Pebble broke and whistle broke, that horse was twined too deep into memory to be left to the care of any characters like Anvil. Bad enough to be at war with a man you couldn't shoot back at, without giving up to him a horse you'd practically raised on a bottle.

The sun was getting warm in his face when he pulled the bronc up and sat looking down on Post Oak through a screen of stunted hackberry. The town looked much the same as he had left it, with the breakfast smoke still curling from a scattering of chimneys and a woman heaving slops from the back porch of Bay Annie's with nothing wrapped around her but a flimsy shift open halfway down the front.

Rambo wasn't interested. His glance conducted a tour of the livery barns and feed lots, going over them carefully and abruptly stopping at Kelley's. Samanthy, still saddled, was tied to a ring at the left of the front doorway. Kelley was hunkered, whittling, on his boots beside another man. There was nobody else in sight in that vicinity except for a couple of urchins shooting marbles off to the right of them.

Peaceful as two sixshooters in the same belt. In fact, too peaceful, Rambo thought, eyeing the stable's bulk suspiciously. He didn't know whether to go down there or not. Anvil had left the horse in sight by way of proving it hadn't been stolen; but he could also have left a couple of hardcases handy to take care of Samanthy's owner should he prove fool enough to come after the gelding.

Rambo, scowling, abruptly got out of the saddle. He took a look at his pistol, and hung fire there a moment, scouting out a way of getting down in one piece and without any punctures. A way, he thought, sighing, whereby he hoped he might do this.

It took him half an hour. Fetched up in a jungle stand of salt cedar rankly lifting behind the three corrals in back of Kelley's barn, he spent another ten minutes carefully watching the place through the filmy screen of blue-green branches. The corral nearest him was empty. The one next beyond held a bunch of scrub stuff eating hay off the ground. He couldn't see what was in the pen next to the stables. Nor any help or lookers.

He ducked through the poles of the nearest

enclosure with an effort at casualness that pattered cold chills up and down his spine. Some of the broncs in the next quit eating to watch him. Halfway across there was a hay fork standing with its tines in the mulch and he leaned against it, sweating, hearing the drone of the flies buzzing round him and the faint, high-pitched voices of the marble-shooting kids.

He felt lank as a gutted snowbird. This was slow work and risky. That fellow out front with Kelley kept gnawing at his thoughts; if he was anyone connected with the Swallowfork ramrod it was a cinch he wasn't out there just to keep that patch of wall shaded. When Rambo finally moved on again he took the hay fork with him. The broncs in the next pen went back to their eating.

He couldn't afford to get them upset. The only alternative was to move into the runway. I got to have that horse, he told himself. He ducked his head then and squeezed between the poles, coming erect in the runway, seeing no one but hearing the dim mumble of voice sounds drifting through the open rear doorway of the barn. Kelley and the watcher still gabbing out front.

He moved forward with the hay fork as though this were a part of his everyday job. He had taken off his spurs before starting down the gulch wall and his boots made little sound as he strode leisurely toward the dark maw of the doorway.

He wasn't six steps away from it when a man came out, tossing him a casual look, commencing to turn for the cross-barred gate of the nearest pen and, abruptly freezing, flinging him a sharper look across a lifted shoulder.

Rambo stopped, too, the hackles standing on his neck as a man's voice viciously said inside the stable, "So I shot the son of a bitch. He was no good to us with a busted hip an' he'd got next to too much to be left around talking. This'll give us another rope on that stinker. You can up the reward. I'll see that Fox pays it."

Anvil's voice!

The man to the right of Rambo went for his gun. Rambo threw the fork at him and, with his nerves shrinking away from the fellow's climbing screech, plunged through the open doorway, crashing headlong into a man coming out.

12

Rambo, gasping, was hurled halfway around by the staggering impact. This was all that saved him, the leaping flame of Anvil's muzzle flash searing his ribs with the bite of hot powder. Before the man could trigger again Steve was at him, wickedly striking with the length of his pistol, feeling the barrel of it crunch against bone. As the ramrod stumbled backward Rambo's swiveling stare, raking the mauve shadows, located George's shape crouched against the wall with a lifting greener.

In that split-second of inactivity, while they eyed each other and the place still throbbed with the dwindling roar of Anvil's fire, he had time to notice how pleased George looked, like it was the first good break he'd got in a lifetime.

A lean grin licked the marshal's teeth, amber stained from tobacco, and the black bore of that shotgun had almost reached focus when Steve dived frantically into the wake of the toppling Swallowfork boss. A grunt of air burst out of those stretched-wide jaws as Rambo's weight dropped across the man's belly; and Rambo's twisting head saw the grin fall away from George's ugly face.

Chagrin, rage and fright stared from the man's gleaming eyes; and then a craziness peered out of them and Rambo, squirming desperately, pulled the ramrod's groaning bulk on top of him. "Drop it, George!"

The marshal hadn't much choice. He let the shotgun slide down his legs to the floor and with the bones of his face standing out like castings raised both hands.

"Get back away from that greener and unbuckle your belt."

The marshal's eyes were wild but he knew better than to argue in the face of that pistol. He let the belt go but said, "You'll never make it, Rambo."

Steve shoved Anvil aside and got up. He knew Kelley and the fellow who'd been squatting there with him were still outside between himself and Samanthy, and he also knew he couldn't go back the way he'd come. They'd cut him down with rifles before he ever got to that bronc. Kelley, even now, was probably dashing up street to get more help; and there was those kids to be thought of, the pair who'd been playing marbles out front—he could almost see the excited look of them now.

He said to George, "Walk ahead of me into the front of this stable. And keep in mind a pair of busted arms won't do your business any good at all."

128

George growled: "You've crowded your luck as far as it will go."

"Maybe."

"You know it. You're a cooked goose the minute you step out of that door." George glared at him, angrily. "I ain't anxious to see you git out of this, bucko; but there's kids outside—got to think of them, too. So here's what I'll do. Pass your solemn word of honor you'll git out of this country an' I'll call off the guns I've got watchin' this place."

Rambo stared so long the marshal finally growled, "Well?"

"I guess I like my way better—"

"Don't look so damn proud! You ain't out of this yet—you ain't no government dick, either. You think I'm aimin' to forgit them three possemen you blasted? You'll trade my way or die here!"

Rambo grinned. "No sale, George."

"You goddam fool! There's half a dozen guns trained on that door right now—"

"I ain't doubting your word, but there's one trained on you, too, and my finger's getting itchy. Get moving, George, or you've had it."

George stamped over to the door. He said loudly across his shoulder, "You'll never reach that horse!"

Rambo's look showed the hardness that had been ground into him. "That's going to be your

129

job, George. I can see Samanthy plain from where I'm standing here in the shadows. Step out there now and untie him, and when you've got that done fetch him back inside here. The first false move you make will be your last one."

The marshal's shape, black against the light outside, appeared to swell like a toad, and then the air rushed out of him. He started, cursing, for the horse, the sunlight bringing out the colors of his clothing and showing the roan of rage that stretched from collar to hairline. Though he listened with every nerve in his motionless body Rambo caught no sounds beyond those made by George's boots. If Kelley had fetched reinforcements they weren't doing any more moving than the man who'd been out there with him.

Rambo's shoulders stirred restlessly. This thing was bigger than he'd guessed. That crooked-nosed marshal was in it up to his ears. He would have let Rambo go, but not very far—not after finding out Steve wasn't packing tin. And Anvil would know that, too, now. The heat would be on in earnest once this bunch got out from under Rambo's gun.

He slanched a glance at the Swallowfork range boss. The ramrod was holding his face in his hands and there was blood dribbling down across the near hand's fingers. "Quit that groaning," Rambo muttered, watching the marshal step up to the bay. The horse had its ears back. Steve called, "Easy, Samanthy," and saw George reach out and jerk the reins from the ring.

He said, "All right, George. Fetch him in here," and heard a board creak behind him.

He ducked and spun like a cat, the pistol in his hand belching flame as he whirled—too late to avoid the shape plunging at him. The man's weight bore him floorward. He fell hard on one hip and heard boots pounding toward them. The man's knee smashed him flat and both the man's hands clamped a death grip on his gun wrist and began thumping it against the rough planks of the flooring.

Rambo rolled and got to his knees and saw the doorway's bright rectangle grow dark with running men; felt the panting breath of the one who had hold of him. With a terrible wrench he came onto his feet and smashed the man against a stall's one-inch sheeting. The man cried out and Rambo hammered his left fist against the fellow's whiskered cheek, guessing this was the man he had recently used that fork on. The fellow's breath was a revolting rattle—an indescribable wheezing, and his grip, though still tenacious, seemed more desperate than it had been. Rambo cracked his noisy head against the stall's partition, sent a knee slamming upward and felt the hands slide away from him.

Through a shouting, yelling gloom black with

shapes George's voice kept yammering, "Git him! Git him!" and beyond those bobbing hats he saw the bay head-tossing bulk of Samanthy with ears pricked forward, nervously snorting and stamping.

Something cuffed at Steve's chaps. Another jerked the cloth round his neck and the air suddenly screamed to the shriek of blue whistlers. He could hear them striking, tearing through the boards behind him; and then the rank aromas of the floor were in his nostrils and he could feel the hoof-scarred planks vibrating with the forward surge of all those spur-clanking boots. He came onto his feet snarling, too wild to feel pain. The buck and leap and deafening roar of his gun was an ecstatic sensation; and when the savage satisfaction of that recoil was denied him he swung the weapon like a club, wading into them, laughing crazily at the expressions of the faces swirling round him.

Exultation rocked him when one of those red faces crumpled and with jaws stretched wide dropped out of sight. He was a wolf at bay inside a ring of yapping curs, still on his feet, still slashing wickedly, but knowing they must prove too many. It was then he remembered to whistle.

Samanthy, trumpeting like a stallion bronc, came tearing into the stable, teeth bared and loose reins flying. It was like an avalanche let loose the way that bay came pounding through them. Ears laid flat against the sides of his head, he came like a wind through a field of standing grain. Nothing could withstand him, no human force could stay him. His swinging head knocked the marshal sprawling against a stanchion, his flailing hoofs passed over another. The rest didn't wait but sprang away in terror; and he was pounding full tilt down the runway when Steve settled into the saddle.

For half an hour Rambo rode with no sensation but relief, content to feel the push of the cool breeze, letting the horse go where he would, too close to exhaustion to think of guiding him. He felt like a man snatched out of the fiery furnace—like Jonah must have felt when God released him from the whale. Content just to be alive.

But then his mind began to rouse with the teeming thoughts which came unbidden; and he pulled himself together, becoming aware of his throbbing shoulder. He stopped Samanthy beside a stream and half fell out of the saddle. His legs, gone numb, refused to hold his weight and he saw the water rush up at him.

That was all he knew. He was never able afterwards to remember whether he fell into the stream or rolled in after blacking out from loss of blood and exhaustion. But he was aware when he got himself up onto the bank that he'd been there a long while. The sun was heeled far over and the breeze cut into him through the drip of his sodden clothing; but he felt a heap better. The wound in his shoulder had quit bleeding and the bite of it now was only a dull ache. The slug had missed the bones, he found, and had gone straight through. He pulled the wipe off his neck and wrung it out, grimacing, afterwards using it to pad the wound as well as he could.

Samanthy was grazing a little way off and looked up at him, curious, as Rambo lurched toward him. The animal looked as though he might be going to play hard to catch but steadied when Rambo spoke to him. Nevertheless, getting into the saddle required effort.

He spent several moments taking stock of his surroundings. He sent the bay striding into the trees when his eye latched onto a landmark he recognized. Evidently his luck had not entirely deserted him. As near as he could judge they weren't over five miles from Barred Circle. Though impatient to get there, in deference to his wound Steve held their pace to a walk.

He was surprised, when he considered it, the marshal's bunch hadn't tracked him down. Probably they reckoned to pick him up at Barred Circle when they came back after Faron; and they'd do no fooling around about it this time.

His thoughts swung again to Anvil's presence in town. How had the ramrod managed to get there ahead of him?

He turned it over in his mind. The man could

have been tipped off; he'd grant them that much, though he found it hard to believe. Uncommon hard—for who besides the cook had seen him? And that in poor light and at considerable distance.

About all Dirty Shirt would have been able to tell Anvil was that some horsebacker had got Fox out of bed tarnashun early, slipping away suspiciously through the grove behind the house while the range boss was riding in at the front. What really baffled Steve, however, was that, if Anvil had got curious, he would have come after him—not cut around him.

He got to thinking then in dead earnest.

A whiskey-jack somewhere in the pines began sending up its raucous call and Steve hauled his chin off his chest to scowl briefly into the blue-lavender of sun-dappled shadows.

He did not hold it very likely they would try an ambush here. Two fizzled jobs were all that any man would care to risk. Loss of face could ruin these bravos. Having watched it work in Golden, Rambo knew the power of laughter. The ramrod had put himself out on a limb. He'd got to bring the next try off or else.

Steve didn't bother to find out where that thought went to. It was Anvil's presence in town which engrossed him. There was an answer to that if he could get his hands on it.

The cook couldn't have told who had been in

the shadows. Only one man could have told the ramrod that; and it had to be the truth to send the range boss larruping back to town without his breakfast.

It didn't make sense no matter what foundation Steve squatted on to view it. Why would Fox tell his range boss it was Rambo who'd been calling? It was Swallowfork's owner who'd himself insisted that Steve get out of there, frightened of what another clash between them might result in.

Rambo wondered in greater bafflement if he'd picked up the wrong impression. *He's coming now. You better drift.* That was what Fox, peering round the shade, had told him. He hadn't said Anvil, but Anvil was the one they'd been wagging their jaws about. And Anvil was the one he'd meant Steve to think was coming. Remembering the desperate timber of the ranchman's voice, it didn't seem possible Fox could have lied to him about it.

The whole deal was twisty as a sackload of snakes. When he'd been talking about those stones, Faron's hoof-kinked memory had seemed to be churning along at a fine rate until he'd got to the place where they'd come off the "soldier's trail." He had claimed that was all he remembered, but Rambo reckoned it was fear that had clamped his mouth shut. And this baffled him too, for had it been fear of Anvil would he have said anything at all?

He must recall to ask Lucie about her outfit's cattle losses. If Anvil was the man Fox had painted him and was making a nice thing out of Overpack steers, might he not also be using Raid's Store as a base for running off Swallowfork critters as well? A smart operator would have a whole chain of stations and it was a damned poor crook who couldn't play both ends from the middle.

Rambo rolled that thought around with his eyes turning brighter.

The sun was long down and night again draped the land when Rambo, for the third time in darkness, rode into the Overpack yard. Seemed like he was getting to be a regular cut-and-run hombre.

The whole left side of him ached like a bad tooth and he felt hot in the head, but there wasn't nothing wrong with his vision and he reckoned a square meal would send a lot of that packing. The wind had blown his shirt dry but his creek-sopped chaps and the pants underneath them still felt glued to his legs when he swung down beside the porch and heard the girl come hurrying through the house in evident excitement.

She pushed open the baggy screen and he wished he could see her face when she cried, "Thank God—I've never been so glad to see anyone!" She caught hold of his hands, pulled him into the lamplit kitchen. "Faron's gone!"

"Faron . . . ?" Rambo stared at her blankly.

"Disappeared! He wouldn't listen—wouldn't hear to waiting till morning. He saddled up right after you left; said he had five years of back work to catch up with. He said he was going out to give the boys a hand with the cattle—"

"You been losing much to rustlers?"

Looking a little surprised, Lucie nodded. "Anyway, when I rode out to the gather this morning he wasn't there. The boys said he hadn't been there, so I took Jay Allison and rode over to Raid's Store. He wasn't there, either, or anybody else." She looked at Rambo anxiously. "What do you suppose has happened to him? Do you think that Swallowfork bunch—"

"Anvil's been too busy. I don't think you've got anything to worry about. If I'm not greatly mistaken your brother has dropped out of sight on his own hook."

"But why would he do that?"

Rambo, staring thoughtfully across her shoulder, said, "He may have been scared those boys would work him over again. Or it could have been that frame the marshal's trying to hang on him." Dropping a hand down alongside his gun butt Rambo stepped a pace away from her and said without preamble: "If he isn't wearing yellow boots that's an uncommon queer place to keep them."

13

The boots walked out from behind the angle of the door and the man who was in them said unabashedly to Lucie, "You want I should do anything about this character?"

The girl's startled look went through astonishment to anger. With spots of brightening color climbing into the forward throw of her cheeks she cried: "What are you doing here?"

The man showed a hard smile. "Just trying to do my job, Miss."

He looked narrow enough to take a bath in a gun barrel. Bony wrists protruded from the too-short sleeves of his shield-fronted shirt and baggy pantalones covered splindling shanks above the blaze of those yellow boots. A bone-handled .45 thrust its corrugated butt from the greasy scuffed holster that was slung at his groin and a battered brown derby completed his attire. Despite this scarecrow appearance his black jowled face was shaved clean as a whipstaff and Rambo, silently watching him, judged this wasn't a fellow he would care to find behind him.

"Your job has nothing to do with this house."

"That's straight, Miss. But after all that digging, and the thoughts that went with it, I figured when

I heard that horse coming in you might be glad of an ace in the hole, so to speak."

Somewhat mollified, but still not liking the idea of this range tramp making free of the house, Lucie said, "We'll let it go for now, but remember after this we keep our aces in the bunkhouse." She looked at him more closely. "It's rather queer I didn't hear you."

"You was in the other room there, pawing through them drawers," the man said.

Lucie's cheeks flamed afresh. "I was hunting a gun—"

"Sure. That's what I figured." His eyes slid over the curves of her shape. "You going to feel all right with this feller in here?"

A dark scowl began to climb Rambo's cheeks, but before he could put his resentment to words Lucie hurriedly said, "Of course. Steve, I want you to meet Tax Manergell—he hired on with us this morning. Tax, this is Steve Rambo; he works for us, too."

Neither man offered to shake hands. Manergell said, with another sly look, "Well, I guess two is company . . ." and ducked his head and walked out.

Rambo waited till his boot sound dropped away across the yard. "That fellow's no kind for you to have around here, Lucie! I wouldn't trust that bucko any farther'n I could heave him. Where did he come from? How do you know he isn't—"

"Are beggars ever choosers? I've tried for months—"

"You're no beggar! Your brother didn't tell all he knows last night; he's probably gone off now to have a look for that Lost Dutchman . . ."

She shook her head, a tired smile reshaping the contours of her cheeks before it faded. "I'm down to grasping straws but I won't fool myself with that one. You didn't know Deke, but you can take it from me if there was gold on this ranch he would have found it long ago." She shook her head again. "Anything that's to be done I'm going to have to do myself."

Almost against his will Rambo said, "I'll do what I can—"

"I know you will, Steve, and I want you to know I'm grateful. It's this shorthandedness that whips me. I didn't tell you this, but that night you were here and Jay Allison rode in we lost another big jag to night riders and Gerry, our range boss, got killed in the brush with them. Jay's riding top screw with only three punchers helping him, trying to round up enough to put a herd on the trail.

"That's about my last hope. If I can't market those cattle before that mortgage falls due—"

"Mortgage!" Rambo stared. "I thought this spread was in the clear—"

"That was my notion, too," Lucie said with mouth tightening. "But it seems the last time

141

Faron went off and got drunk he got roped into a card game and put Barred Circle in hock to the bank in order to pay off his losses. It was a short term note and it's due in three weeks—"

"How much did he borrow?"

"Eight thousand dollars."

They considered each other. Rambo finally said: "Some card game!" and stared somberly past her, seeing his sister and hearing the tramp of rain on the roof. He scrubbed bruised knuckles against the side of his face. "That's hard to swallow. I know one thing, though. Sure as God made fish and tadpoles, if they've got your brother's name on a paper—"

He broke his words off with a start of surprise. "You ever see this note?"

She shook her head.

"And good reason," Steve muttered. "There never was any—that's why they rigged this bank-breaking deal! To cover themselves against investigation! Why, it's plain as plowed ground— if Faron ever goes on trial we'll find there was nothing else taken; nothing missing but that note!"

Her eyes came up and queerly met his glance. "You're forgetting Rammickey."

"No, they had to kill Rammickey. Here's the way they'll argue. Barred Circle's been losing a lot of cattle to rustlers. This spread is about strapped. Faron, knowing he couldn't pay that

142

note off in time, stuck up the bank thinking if he could get and destroy that note—"

"It doesn't matter. The thing is done, and now they'll put a price on his head. And if I don't get a herd to the chutes at Florence . . . That's why I hired this fellow. He's tough enough looking—"

"He's tough clear through. This thing is too pat! After all these weeks you've been trying to hire punchers that fellow didn't just happen—"

"He said he'd heard Barred Circle was short-handed. He's been down below the line, selling sewing machines out of Taxaco; the revolution ran him out. Lost everything he had, he said—"

"Yeah, he says a lot of things in addition to his prayers. Sewing machines!" Rambo snorted. "You get a look at his eyes?"

He commenced a turn around the table. The walls of the room abruptly wavered and canted, expanding and contracting like the jaws of a mudcat. Rambo's knees got weak and shook uncontrollably. He scrubbed his cheek with a fist again. "That fellow's a killer—"

"Steve!" she cried, springing toward him. Where the dizziness had stopped him the lamp's yellow glow revealed the stain below his shoulder, the sodden condition of his chaps. "You're wet—and you've been hurt!"

"Nothing a little grub and rest won't mend," he told her gruffly.

But she got his shirt off anyway and made

143

him sit in a chair while she fetched rags and heated water. Rambo eyed her testily. "Hell's gilded hinges! Guy would think I was a stretcher case the way you're carryin' on." She started pouring broth into a heating pan and he growled, "Never mind that hogwash! Toss a steak in that skillet and slice up some spuds and bermudas, something a hungry man can get his teeth into. All that's wrong with me is I've turned soft from lack of grub."

She put a bottle of oil of salt on the table, laid a hand across his forehead and looked at him, prettily worried. "You've got a little fever—"

"That's from being so close to you, I guess."

She got the cloths and the water. She didn't smile back at him.

"A hole like that isn't a thing to make a joke about."

"I'll be good as new, come morning. Soon's you get this thing plugged I'll go rub down Samanthy—"

"You'll stay right in that chair until I tell you to get off it!"

Rambo looked at her quizzically. "Yes, ma'am."

"I'll put up your horse. After you get that broth down you'll get into Faron's bed—"

"Not on your life! I'll bed down in the bunk-house like the rest of the hired help." He didn't aim to give Manergell's jaw cause to clack. Bad enough having a fellow like him in the outfit without giving him the notion the spread was nursing a cripple. Steve said as much to Lucie while she was finishing up the bandage.

She said, "I'll wash this scarf out for you. Better let me wash and patch that shirt, too. I think one of Deke's should be a pretty good fit." She got a bowl and a spoon and some crackers from the cupboard.

"You expect a man to keep his strength up on this stuff?"

"Just eat it," she said; "I'll give you steak for breakfast." She went off and came back with a gray flannel shirt. "How did you get shot?"

Steve told her. He reckoned, the way she looked, she sensed the gap in his story, but he didn't want to tell her about going back to Swallowfork; set as she was on Fox being the bad wolf of this piece he was afraid any mention of that business at the window would only serve to confirm her suspicions. He wasn't yet willing to admit she might be right. He wanted time to put more thought on it. After all, it was entirely possible Anvil *had* ridden in to the ranch. Until he knew more he decided to keep it to himself.

Post Oak hummed like a wood-boring beetle.

All over town folks reshuffled the facts and came up with the answers which best suited their natures. Across back fences worried women compared notes above the din of feuding off-spring. In the mercantile, the bakeshop, along plank walks and in the bars of deadfalls, men congregated with vigorous gestures, dispensing guesses like gospel before hurrying off to augment other groups of head-shaking wind millers. Long before they tired of it the recent battle at Drake's stable bade fair to outshine the O.K. Corral fight at Tombstone.

The barber told the butcher he couldn't think what the world was coming to. The baker told the hotel man if things got much worse he was all for calling the Cavalry in. A cattle buyer from Prescott took the next stage out and was forced to ride in the rack with the luggage, the belly of the coach was so crammed with departing drummers. Tanner's gun shop did a land-rush of business and oily Jeb Driscal, who owned the furniture store and did a sideline in undertaking, rubbed his hands and smiled.

Crooked Nose George recruited ten extra deputies and Rufus Coffin, M.D., told the man who ran the pool parlor that it looked like Swallowfork was about set to skin its rabbit.

The following morning the new hand, Tax Manergell, was first to get dressed in the Barred Circle bunkhouse. This was not a process of any great duration. He swung bony shanks over the side of his bunk, clapped on his battered derby with a couple of sidelong looks at Rambo, got the bone-handled pistol from under his ticking, strapped on his cartridge belt and thrust his feet down into the odiferous sweat-damp leather of those gaudy yellow boots.

When he'd tramped outside with a deal of raucous hawking, Rambo carefully got out of his own bunk. For obvious reasons he had not stripped to the buff last night, either, but he had taken off his pants. Getting into them now was a task needing patience and pulling on his cold boots made him grind his teeth in anguish, what with the way his left shoulder had stiffened. He worked the arm gingerly, scowling as he kneaded lame muscles; and he didn't go out until Manergell came back.

He felt a lot brisker after splashing his face.

Lucie'd got a lamp lit in the kitchen by this time and he went back inside and turned up their own. Manergell was hunched on a bunk cleaning his pistol. Now he tossed the rag away, refilled the cylinder and replaced it.

They eyed each other like a couple of strange dogs. Then Manergell laughed. "Better look at yours, too. I mighta pulled the loads while you was pounding your ear."

Rambo let that ride.

Manergell said, "Pretty flossy chunk of chicken," and jerked his chin toward the house.

Rambo's cheeks showed heat. Black eyes

colder than the bucket he had washed in, he said bleakly: "She's a lady, and you damn well better remember it."

"When you get under their flounces there ain't much difference."

Rambo looked at him carefully, then his teeth showed a little, too. He had to bear down hard on his impulse but he had been around enough to know when he was being maneuvered. For some reason undiscoverable to him this bleach-eyed customer was trying to prod his goat. He said, "You ready to eat now?"

"Feelin' kind of faint, eh?"

Rambo matched his grin, but it took effort. "I never argue with a drunk or with a gent that's got a gun in his lap."

Manergell laughed and thrust the gun into leather. "Always take the measure of any buck I have to work with. Old habit of yours, taking a bath with your chaps on?"

Steve didn't follow the fellow's glance to the bunk where last night he had hung up his batwings to dry. He reckoned they'd be stiff enough to stand by themselves. But the chaps weren't any issue. He kept his eyes on Manergell.

The thin man got up with another taunting grin. "I can see well enough why he pinned his hopes on you. When you're going to plant a spy it always pays to plant a smart one."

A cold chill got off its hocks and commenced

to work up Rambo's spine. "What are you getting at?"

"You denyin' you come from Swallowfork?"

Rambo said, "Miss Overpack knows about that—"

"Does she understand why you come into this country?"

"Maybe you'd better chew that a little finer."

Manergell laughed and set off across the yard.

All during breakfast Rambo covertly studied him, wondering if their tracks had crossed before; wondering too, if they hadn't, why the man was bent on crowding him. Was this simply a case of two fast guns or was there more behind it than the man had disclosed? He couldn't place the face or voice, was practically certain they'd no previous acquaintance. How had the man found out he'd come from Swallowfork?

There were plenty of ways he could have latched onto that. Anvil could have told him. So could George, the Post Oak marshal. Either one could have sent him out here. He might be the saddle tramp he looked but, in his line, he was an expert. The gunsmoke smell was ground deep into him. Those yellow boots were a trademark, the measure of his pride.

George could still have sent him but somebody else was paying for his keep—someone other than Lucie who had hired him because she was desperate. Anvil?

149

Lucie—had she pushed the thought to this point—would have said it was Forko Fox; but Rambo, remembering her background, was inclined to discount this. He hadn't yet decided Fox had lied to him yesterday morning by implying it was his range boss who'd been riding into the yard. He still thought it might have been.

Yet, while Rambo wasn't accepting the girl's estimate of Fox, he felt a deal less ready to put reliance in his own. He didn't quite know what to think. Fox might be the devil she thought him. Against this all Rambo had to offer was his own unbolstered conviction to the contrary. There was too much smoke and he didn't think Fox was that good an actor.

Why, for instance, if Fox wasn't on the level, would he have admitted Anvil's hold on him? And, if that were pure invention, why go to so much bother? To clear himself of complicity in the matter of Barred Circle? To use Steve Rambo for a catspaw?

Rambo smiled derisively. It would be cheaper and simpler to send Steve packing and then, if he proved troublesome, to have him knocked off. *Unless he also wanted to rid himself of Anvil.* But there were less dangerous ways than hiring Rambo to watch him, particularly if—as their talk had indicated—Fox believed Steve to be a government agent. Or had Fox been throwing sand there, too?

Rambo reckoned he was getting in over his ears. No workable scheme would be so elaborate; the whole thing was preposterous. To believe the ranchman guilty of inspiring the plight of the Overpacks—and then to fetch Rambo into it as he'd been fetched in—you would have to give the Swallowfork owner some motive far greater than plain greed or hatred.

Steve turned his thoughts back to Manergell. He may have missed some roadsign in regard to Fox, overlooked something not too clearly apparent on the surface, but he understood Manergell's kind from past experience. This fellow was plumb cultus—*hombre malo puro*, a gunhawk who would kill without compunction or hesitation. The only question Rambo pondered with regard to Manergell's presence was the vital one of whom. Had he come here to bump off Steve or to rub out Faron Overpack—or both? He may even have been told to break up Lucie's trail herd, but a hardcase of his caliber wouldn't have been sent here just for that. Watching the fellow's eyes Rambo would sooner have sat with a rattlesnake—you knew what the rattlesnake would do.

Lucie said, as Manergell pushed back his chair, "I want you both to ride straight out to the herd. You can tell Jay Allison I've just put you on."

Manergell nodded and, getting up, reached for the makings—with his left hand, Rambo noticed.

Lucie's glance uncertainly considered Steve for a moment and he could sense her hesitation. She said abruptly to the thin man, "While you're roping out a horse, suppose you saddle one for Rambo, too. I've a couple of things to say to him—alone," she added pointedly.

Manergell grinned, bold eyes going over her. He stuck the quirly in his face and scooped up the battered derby. "I'll take that bay," Rambo called as he was crossing the porch.

He was glad he'd put Samanthy up last night himself.

Lucie said, "How do you feel?"

"I'll manage," he nodded. He listened to the gunhawk's boots. "Ever consider hiring a wild bunch?"

"You mean brush crawlers? Outlaws?"

"Yeah."

She swept a startled breath into her lungs and said, "No." Her eyes dug at him. "Wouldn't that be crazy?"

"Probably." He kept thinking of that gunhawk. Of Faron and Fox and the Swallowfork ramrod. And back of these shadows was the darker face-less gloom of the man whose lost tracks had pulled him into this. "We've got our tails in a crack and it's cut stick or else."

14

"You mean we can't stay here?"

"We've got price tags on us, your brother and me. They'll be made stiff enough to fill these hills with bounty hunters. We've got to keep moving. You can't stay here by yourself. If it's gold that crowd's after—"

"But there's no gold on this ranch!"

"You may have the right of that, but so long as they think there is you've got to cut and run with the rest of us. God above, girl—do you reckon I want you treated like Faron?"

She stared at him wordless, then came into his arms.

He put her away from him. "We've got to fight fire with fire—"

"But outlaws, Steve! We couldn't trust them."

"We can't trust anyone." *Not even ourselves!* He thought bitterly. "It's dog eat dog from here on out. We take what we can, and wherever, or we go under."

She frowned, considering him, finally shaking her head. "I've lived all my life in this country. I know it's harsh, often brutal; but there's nobody in it that would harm a woman."

"Your brother put his hands on a woman. What

153

reason you got to think this Manergell won't? That fellow's no house cat. He was in here last night, standing back of that door. And you didn't even know it. Get your eyes open, Lucie!"

"You don't imagine—"

"That bravo isn't here by accident. I want you out at the cow camp. By noon at the latest. Case I'm not there, stay in sight of your crew." He said grimly: "I don't want you alone with that Manergell, ever."

She drew a long breath, blue eyes dark, unreadable. "If you feel that way about him perhaps I'd better let him go."

"I don't want him to go; I want him where I can watch him." He studied her a moment. "With this fellow you're a side issue. Like that herd your crew's building."

Her eyes narrowed a little. "You think he's after Faron?"

"It doesn't matter who he's after. I don't want him driven into the rimrocks. If we can skin by without trouble until this shoulder gets better—"

"You're playing with fire."

"Sure I'm playing with fire! What do you think would happen if you tried to get rid of him? We'd have it right then or he'd go into the brush."

Lucie said quietly, "What do you want me to do?"

"Tell me where I can find a few hardcases. Then keep out of his way until I get on my feet."

Rambo found the horses ready and waiting. Samanthy was standing on trailing reins. The new hand was shaping a cigarette, comfortably anchored in his saddle with a knee around the horn. "Love an' kisses," he said, grinning.

Rambo paid no attention to him, overtly at least. He loosened the cinch and squeezed a hand under the blanket. There were no wrinkles in it. He pulled on the trunk strap.

"Hunting sand burrs?" Manergell asked. "I could've shoved a few under it if I'd known you was partial to 'em."

"Let's go," Rambo said, and got into the saddle, conscious of the man's mocking scrutiny. He hoped the pain that haul gave his shoulder wasn't showing.

"You know where they're at?"

"We'll find them," Rambo said. He set as slow a pace as he dared, not wanting to rip open that wound if he could help it.

They came up on the herd with the sun an hour high. Two punchers were holding it, slowly riding circle. These eyed the newcomers suspiciously. One of them rode up with a rifle across his pommel. "Lookin' for somethin'?"

"Allison," Rambo said, and the man, still far from satisfied, allowed they'd probably find him in the second gulch. He jerked his head northwest and they rode on, moving at a walk till they were clear of the herd.

"Butter wouldn't melt in his mouth," Manergell said.

"They've been having a lot of trouble."

Manergell sniffed. "They dunno what trouble is."

Rambo's mouth corners tightened. A quarter mile farther on they passed the first gulch and, ten minutes later, breasting the mouth of the second, heard cattle coming. They pulled off to the side and watched three brindle steers break out of it and, hard on their heels, two blacks and a tan. Shod hoofs clanged on rock and two riders appeared, wheeling their horses to a stop, reaching for rifles.

"No call for fireworks," Rambo said. "We're hunting Allison."

The two men traded looks and the smaller rode off, hazing the cattle toward the herd. "Speak your piece," Allison said.

He was a rawboned fellow in a chin-strapped hat with a grizzle of wiry beard on his cheeks. His right hand lay close to the grip of his pistol. His pale eyes were cold and bright with suspicion.

Rambo supplied their names, explaining they'd been hired and told to show up here for work. Allison's hostile expression did not thaw in the slightest.

"All right," he said curtly. "Ride along down

this draw an' start working the next canyon. Never mind the young stuff. All I want is beef. Push down—"

"Just a minute," Rambo cut in. "I've got some further instructions—"

"From Miz' Overpack or Forko Fox?"

Manergell grinned. Rambo said, "Take it easy." He fished a folded paper from the pocket of his shirt and held it out, but the acting range boss made no move to take it.

"Paper's cheap. About as cheap as hot air."

Rambo, staring into those frosty eyes, said, "You'd know her writing if you saw it, wouldn't you?"

"Can't say that I would. Nor I ain't fool enough to try."

Rambo, scowling, thrust the paper back in his pocket. He couldn't rightly blame Allison for the stand he was taking, but time was running out on them. It was infuriating to think that this old codger's shrewdness and his natural suspicion might occasion the loss of the very thing he was bent on protecting—the precious herd the girl was counting on to keep the bank from grabbing Barred Circle. Anvil, after that fracas in town, would be hog-wild for hair by this time.

Everything was piling up and here they stood swapping jaw when they ought to be lining this herd out for Florence. Rambo said, "We've got to get these cattle out of here. Faron hasn't shown up and there's a price on his scalp. They'll—"

"Seems to me I heard there's a price on yours, too. I wasn't born yesterday, Rambo."

Steve tried to dig up some line that would sway him. "If we went over to the herd you could have those boys keep us covered with their saddle guns while—"

"You're not going near that herd. You might's well make up your mind to it."

"Man, use your head! Lucie'll be out here this noon—"

"Then we'll just wait for her," Allison said, "an' she can tell me herself what she wants done about it."

Rambo, riled more than ever by Manergell's grin, snarled bitterly, "It could be too late by then. The time to get them moving's right now. That Post Oak marshal—"

"He in the gang, too?" Allison rested his hand on the butt of his sixshooter. Manergell's eyes showed the flatness of fish scales but the Barred Circle boss kept his hard stare on Rambo.

"You don't look no better to me than you did last time. Foolin' women comes easy to some kinds of skunks, but I don't have to see a frog to know its croak when I hear it. If you want to chase cows chase some out of that canyon. But stay clear of that herd or you will damn quick get planted."

"Come on," Rambo growled, hazing Manergell

away from him; yet not until they'd covered a full two-twenty yards did his heart drop back out of the way of his breathing. He was forced to give Allison a kind of grudging admiration, but he could cheerfully have shaken the old man's teeth loose. That hard shine hadn't yet gone out of Manergell's stare, and he kept twisting around as though half minded to go back.

"Hell with him," Rambo said. "Let's see how many we can jump out of these rocks. More we can add to that bunch the better the pickings when we take 'em away from him."

Manergell's stare came around like a gun snout. Rambo thought for a second this was going to be it, and then the fellow's lips peeled back from his teeth. "You declarin' in on it?"

Rambo said, "I might as well. How big a slab would I get?"

The hard eyes studied him above that twisted grin. "Ain't you changin' your tune?"

"Not enough to make much difference. Did you think I was in this for forty and found? I had ideas of my own but how far would I get trying to buck the bull moose?"

They rode a few lengths in silence. "Let it drag for awhile," Manergell said finally. "I'll put some thought on it. Mebbe I'll come up with somethin' better than a cut."

Rambo nodded, not fooled any more than he supposed the other was.

Any kind of truce, at this point, looked better than action. His grazed ribs were on the mend now and his shoulder wasn't gouging him as bad as he'd expected, but the longer he could keep this fellow on leash the better. He hoped at least he might manage to keep him immobilized until Lucie could straighten things out with Jay Allison.

Meanwhile there were these cows to chouse. The more critters they could get thrown into that gather the better Lucie's chances for coming out on top. He wasn't kidding himself on that score either.

They worked with a will, even Mangerell appearing to be engrossed with the business, shunting cattle down the canyon to Allison's pickup men below. Three of the steers Steve jumped out of the brush hadn't ever been caught in a roundup before. They were wilder than rabbits and he was glad there was no call to put a rope on these *ladinos*.

The work, hot though it was, didn't keep Steve's thoughts from juning. High on his agenda was a projected visit to Thief River, where the girl had said he might expect to find the kind of tough hands he was after, desperate men who might be persuaded to the plan that was shaping up in his head. He remembered what she'd said about no one being at Raid's Store and he wondered some more about Manergell, what his stake was in this and what stakes could be offered on behalf of Barred Circle to that chaparral breed holed up at Thief River.

His thinking touched George and coasted down a long spiral, recalling how someone had told him the man had once been Anvil's range boss. He wondered how Anvil's head felt this morning. Not bad enough, probably, to throw him off his feed.

Where was Faron Overpack? How much more did the fellow know than he had told the other night? Was he off now hunting that chimerical bonanza or was he holed up someplace chatter-teethed with fright?

A pusillanimous sort, from what the girl had told Steve, even when he was normal; and Rambo had no way of guessing if he were normal now or not. He was certainly scared about something—scared maybe Steve would try to beat them out of that cockeyed mine!

His thoughts swung back to Lucie as was their habit here of late with all too frequent regularity. He sensed how full she was of hidden riches, and remembrance of their closeness when he'd put his arm around her came to mock and haunt him. She was one who'd not take love lightly, holding back the things she felt for a man who could command the high fidelity that was in her. For that one, Steve mused wistfully, she could be the last page in the book.

It was noon when they knocked off and followed the last jag toward the circled herd. Two of Allison's crew took the steers off their hands and one of these called, "Better git over there an' get some before Jay throws it out."

Allison was squatting alongside the fire and got onto his feet as they pulled up by the wagon. He took a last swig of coffee and set his cup on the tailgate. "Light down an' grab some," he said, eyeing them dourly.

"Where's the boss?" Rambo asked, and the codger's lips rolled back off his teeth in a contempt too plain to be hidden. Not bothering to answer, he stepped around to squat down in the shade of the fly and, with the scorn still showing, started building a smoke.

Rambo got stiffly out of the saddle, conscious of Manergell's watching stare, and found a plate and a cup and a bent-handled spoon. The plate and cup he filled at the fire and then set back to cool on the tailgate while he slipped Samanthy's bridle and loosened the cinch. He took his grub over and hunkered down in the thin shade not far from Allison.

Manergell lifted his derby and ran his wipe around the edge of damp hair, then he saddle-cramped over and loosened his own cinch. But he left the bit where it was and made the horse chew grass around it. He heaped a plate with beans and sowbelly and got himself a mug of

162

coffee, unabashed by the unfriendly atmosphere.

When he was done Rambo scrubbed his tin plate bright with sand and wiped out his cup with a twist of grass. Though his face stayed blank as a poker chip, anxiety was beginning to sharpen its claws and he watched for a dust with mounting disquiet.

"Mebbe somethin' come up," Manergell offered, still chewing.

Rambo let the thought ride. But when another half hour slid by with no sign of her he got suddenly up, throwing away his smoke and saying to the old man, "I'm going to take a look around."

There was a pistol in Allison's hand when he arose and nothing on his face but that cold scorn honed bright and edgy. "Take this other snake along with you, an' when you get away from here don't bother about comin' back."

15

With noon less than two hours away Lucie Anna, mindful of the promise exacted by Rambo, had got into a fresh waist and riding skirt and was reaching the coiled rope down from her saddle with Chunk, her favorite among the horses left at the ranch, speculatively regarding her from behind the peeled poles, when hoof sound pulled her head around.

She saw the five horsebackers entering the yard and, though she recognized the Swallowfork ramrod, chose to ignore him—which was mistake number one.

Rope in hand she approached the barred gate of the corral, watching the mock terror of the horse instead of Anvil, thus compounding folly.

She slipped through the bars. Her first loop missed the snorting gelding's head by inches. Flinging up its heels the clowning animal rushed to the pen's far side, loudly blowing through dilated nostrils. With rope recoiled Lucie stalked him warily, enjoying as much as he did this sly game he loved to play.

A pair of the Swallowfork hands swapped grins. Anvil, cheeks dark with anger, got out of his saddle and, pausing by the forge shop, picked up a length of half inch pipe.

Lucie got Chunk on the second try. He let his breath out mournfully. Shaking himself vigorously he let her haul him in.

There was one other horse in the pen besides Chunk, a tired old pensioner that Faron sometimes used. Lucie knew this one wouldn't bother to bolt. Taking down the bars she led Chunk over to her saddle. She slipped the bit in his mouth and, taking off the rope, left him on dropped reins while she went back and put up the bars.

She got her blanket, shook it out and, when she turned, found Anvil facing her. "Mebbe you don't hear good, Miss. I told you to quit foolin' with that bronc and pay attention."

Lucie raked him with disdainful eyes, stepped around him to put the blanket on the horse and, still without speaking, went after her saddle.

Anvil watched with a brightening fury.

When he was around his own headquarters and got into a mood he couldn't take out on anyone, it had become his invariable habit to start honing up his skinning knife. He didn't have his whetstone with him but he had that length of pipe in his hand and his knuckles turned white with the grip he put on it.

He didn't say another word. He stood there glaring while she smoothed out the blanket and settled the leather, his mean little shoebutton eyes glinting wickedly as she caught up the cinch and ran the latigo through its ring. He waited while she bumped the air from the horse, took up the slack and hauled the end of the strap through the last twist she'd made in it.

He waited till she straightened and was facing him again and then he fetched that length of half inch pipe down between the gelding's ears like a maul.

The horse collapsed in its tracks; and that was when Lucie made her third and final mistake. A braided quirt hung from her wrist and, outraged beyond endurance, she leaped at him and swung it. The knotted thongs in a whistling arc laid open his cheek from ear to chin.

His hat fell off and rolled in a circle.

His bald head gleamed in the sun like it was varnished, and blood from the open gash appeared and made his face look gray as wood ash. He didn't snarl or say one word but the pipe in his hands was slowly bent till it looked like a pretzel and, if ever a man's eyes blazed malevolence, his did.

He tossed the mangled iron away from him and looked at the blood rolling off his chin and walked over to his horse and got into the saddle. Only then did he speak. In a hoarse, half strangled whisper he ordered three of his men to ransack the house and fetch out every personal belonging they could locate. "Pictures, clothes, keepsakes an' such truck—don't leave a goddam thing."

They were back inside seven minutes, arms loaded with a heterogeneous assortment of odds and ends; a lace shawl that had been the pride of Lucie's mother dangled from a hip pocket of one of the burly ruffians. Under a load of miscellaneous wearing apparel another fetched out two framed portraits; this one had a pair of bloomers pulled on over his brush-clawed chaps and with a simpering smirk called, "Fawncy seein' you 'ere, Gwindy!"

Displaying with his arms filled all the grace of a waddling elephant, he attempted a pirouette but stepped on a dragging coatsleeve and went down like a diving porpoise.

His companions guffawed but the clown in the bloomers, affecting much concern, pawed frantically through the mound of clothing to come up finally, loudly sighing, with the pair of framed canvasses. He appeared to wipe them off with great tenderness; then, abruptly turning them so the faces showed, said, "Guess which one's the lady."

Charcoal whiskers adorned both portraits.

Lucie said, "My brother will kill you for that."

The one in the bloomers shuddered. Anvil, with a snot rag pressed to his cheek, said: "Gwindy, there's a axe in the forge shop. Git it."

When the man reappeared with it, a hefty double-bitted one, the Swallowfork boss ordered,

"Knock down all the doors an' then start bustin' out them winders. Shenk, you an' Solly fetch out the best of that furniture. An' hurry it up—we ain't got all day."

When the three had gone Lucie started for her mother's picture.

Anvil snarled, "Keep away from that!" and, when it was plain she meant to ignore him, said "Krantz, take ahold of her."

The fourth hand dropped off his horse and caught her running. When she tried to fight him off the fellow cuffed her across the face and, seizing her bodily, came back with her kicking across his shoulder. "Truss her up," Anvil growled through the racket Gwindy was making in the house with his axe.

Krantz enjoyed that plainly. When he got her wrists lashed in front of her with piggin string Anvil's eyes considered her balefully. "Go throw a hull on that crowbait."

Krantz moved into the corral and saddled the pensioner.

"Never mind that bridle—put her rope around his neck. Now fetch him over here."

When Krantz came up with the ancient gelding the other three hands were just about finished. They had the best of the heirloom pieces Deke Overpack had hauled from Louisiana stacked up by the pile of scattered clothing. Gwindy, discarding his axe, commenced rummaging the drawers of a rosewood desk. He got a dogeared album from the drawer above the kneehole and, riffling the pages, called, "Full of kid pitchers, brats in diapers an'—Cripes! Here's one of the ol' woman! Musta been a pippin—"

Anvil said to Krantz, "Shove that stick between her elbows an' put her on the horse. Tie her hands to the horn an' turn him around. I want her to git a good look at this. Shenk, stuff some of the clothes under them furnishin's an' throw on that book Gwindy's got an' touch a match to it."

When the blaze began to roar he showed the girl his yellowed fangs. "How you like that, missy? You gittin' thawed out any?"

Rambo and Manergell weren't over a couple of miles from headquarters when they both caught the odor of smoke and pulled up. "Don't smell like no cook fire," the thin man said. "Got a varnish tang to it and a stink like burnin' wool."

Rambo put spurs to the bay without answering. Manergell, coming up on steel a length behind him, eyed Steve's back consideringly with spread fingers hovering scarce an inch above his gun butt. But, if he were contemplating using it, something must have changed his mind. He took the hand away and let it rest against his thigh.

Rambo stopped the bay again a scant ten minutes later on the crest of a ridge where he waited for Manergell, on the slower horse, to catch him. They had a good view of the yard from there and when the new hand came up Steve held silent for a moment, abruptly asking, "What do you make of it?"

"Looks like there's been a fire, all right." The thin man's horse was breathing hard. "You reckon that bronc down there's been shot?"

Rambo put Samanthy down the slope and pulled into the yard, studying the ground without leaving the saddle even though Manergell swung down for closer inspection. Steve left him at it, slowly walking his horse past the house's broken windows, bleakly seeing what had happened inside and finally stopping the bay beside the still smoldering ends of charred wood ringing the blackened ground between the smithy and Chunk's dead body.

Manergell walked over. "Five guys. They took the girl."

"Yeah." Rambo said from the saddle, "Your bunch, wasn't it?"

Manergell started to speak and then looked up at him sharply. Silence clamped down with neither man stirring so much as an eyelash. For perhaps five seconds they stayed as rigid as shapes on display in a wax works. Then Manergell grinned. "If you believe that, Steve, why don't you go for your pistol?"

"I'm probably not in your class, for one thing," Rambo answered, "and I've still got hopes of being invited to throw in with you. For the big kill," he added, forcing stiff lips to smile.

There was a bright curiosity in the thin man's lifted stare. "Go ahead," he said, "you're doin' the talking. Whereabouts are you fittin' me into this deal and—assuming that there is one—how would it advantage me to cut a fresh hand in?"

"The handouts grow on bushes when two outfits jump for each other's throats. When a whole range gets roped into it the take is bound to be multiplied. If the thing was handled with the right sort of care a really smart gent could come out of this thing with the whole durn country in his hip pocket."

Manergell chewed on his lip, eyes giving nothing away. "And where do you come into it?"

"I have Miss Overpack's confidence," Steve said. "If you've got your sights set on the Lost Dutchman mine, that ought to be worth something to you. And I'm a smoother hand than Anvil."

Something back of Manergell's stare swelled and shifted and his eyes came alive and went brightly narrow. "What's the Swallowfork ram-rod got to do with it?"

Rambo pushed surprise into his look. "You're wanting me to think that bunch has played you for a sucker?"

"Talk plain," Manergell rasped with the eyes staring out of him like two holes in a blanket.

"You should know Anvil's habits a heap better than me. You say five men grabbed the girl. I won't deny it. But I'm telling you one of those five was Anvil." He swept his left hand toward a patch of scarred ground. "He was riding that splayfooted dun with the blaze."

The thin man looked at the tracks. "You've got damn good eyes if you can say who was ridin' it—"

"Look over there. See that piece of twisted pipe? You know anybody else that could bend pipe like that? Go over and look at that hide. The girl had just got him saddled. Whoever knocked him down must have used that pipe. See those scuffed places there? That's where the girl jumped him. There's where his hat fell off—see the mark of it? She probably hit him with her quirt."

They looked at each other for a couple of moments. Manergell said skeptically, "If you can read all that tell me where that damn cub has got to."

"Faron? I can't tell you that. But Anvil and the girl aren't over an hour away from us now."

Manergell eyed him for a long thought-filled second. Then shrugged bony shoulders. "All right. It's a deal. I'll cut you in. Why'd he grab her?"

"I read tracks, not minds," Rambo said with a frown.

"Make a guess."

"I think he's after that gold. On his own hook. If he hasn't got Faron the kid's probably hiding. He might figure grabbing the girl would pull him into the open. Or suck you or me into some trap he's devising."

"Sounds kind of far-fetched," Manergell said. "Looks like to me he'd be more apt to try to force her into marryin' him. That way he'd be settin' pretty; he's probably carryin' her to town—"

"I can track him," Rambo said.

"I thought you figured that's what he's wantin' you to do?"

"Might not be expecting me so quick. I could find out where he's taking her. I could meet you here some time tonight—"

"You got all the answers, ain't you."

"Not all of them—"

"Why do you think the girl's brother's hiding?"

"He's the key. Anvil worked him over with a quirt the other day. He didn't get what he was after but it knocked some sense back into the kid—it was the night George's posse came out to collar him for that bank job. After the kid chased them off with that greener he was different. He let on he'd been with his old man the day Deke found the stone horse head—one of the things that's supposed to be a clue to that mine. Then his eye lit on me and he shut up like a clam. He disappeared the same night. About as soon as I pulled out of here."

Manergell's voice turned crisp with decision. "All right. You go after them. Keep back out of sight and find out where they've taken her. You ought to get back before morning. I'll meet you here. In the stable." He scowled a moment in thought. "Make a sound like a mockingbird. If everything's clear I'll give the call back to you."

16

Rambo followed sign for two solid hours that would stand in his memory as the blackest two hours he'd ever known in his life. Brought face to face with what she meant to him now he was compelled to acknowledge that nothing else mattered without he had Lucie. The belatedness of this discovery hung the bitter truth of it around his neck with all the soul-searching weight of the Mariner's albatross for, with each passing mile if not indeed with each passing moment, the tracks of Anvil's passage got fainter and fewer.

He was in rock country now, in that barren wilderness of shale and broken ledgerock that spread its desolation for more than twenty square miles between the three red hills and LaBarge Canyon south of the Salt River. He blamed himself now for not having insisted that she accompany them this morning, though he was forced to admit—with Manergell in the deal—this might not have made any appreciable difference. The bony gunhawk, he was convinced, had not turned up at Barred Circle by chance. And what that yellow-booted hardcase knew about sewing machines could be thrust in your eye without ever feeling it.

But the fellow was no run-of-mill gunslick. He was as different from Colorado as the night is from day; he might even be the brains behind this deal, Steve thought. Certainly, whether he'd come to break up that drive or put the skids under Faron and Rambo, he hadn't taken cards to give any help to Lucie Overpack.

The notion occurred to Rambo he might even be Deuce Kramer. He didn't seem the type Steve's sister would have gone for; still he did have a kind of hard confidence and polish that must have been felt by Lucie or she never would have hired him. Remembrance of his references to the girl made Steve's hot blood burn.

Rambo's talk hadn't drawn him, and probably hadn't fooled him any more than he'd fooled Steve with that lying promise of a cut. One thing Rambo's jawing may have done though—he certainly hoped so—was plant a few suspicions in Manergell's mind concerning Anvil. Whichever of them happened to be the big cheese it would be all to the good if he could get them squabbling, and he had a strong hunch the wiry Manergell hadn't known a thing about that business of Faron and Anvil. If the gold angle was something being soft-pedalled by the Swallowfork ramrod there might be some fur flying now this bird had got next to it.

These thoughts came in spite of him, but the most of Steve's attention was concerned with his job of unraveling sign and this he was finding to be steadily more difficult.

The first hard choice he'd had to make had confronted him an hour ago when two of the six sets of tracks he had been following branched away from the rest in the direction of Fort Apache. Rambo elected to stick with Anvil's dun even when, presently, another horse had turned aside, lunging off toward that Swallowfork line-camp where Anvil and Colorado had thrown down on Brick.

Steve found it maddening to think he might have passed up the best bet by not sticking to Manergell. If the thin man was rodding this he'd know where Lucie was headed for and might be cutting straight over there now while Anvil gave Steve the slip in this rock maze.

Steve had begun to sweat then and he was sweating in grim earnest when the fourth horse quit and left but two ahead of him. One of these last was Anvil's dun but that didn't prove Forko's ramrod was on it and, even if he were, Lucie might not still be with him—she might have been with the first pair to turn off. She could have been mounted on either of the others.

And then, on a dark sheen of malpais that covered three acres, the tracks vanished entirely. He spent another half hour grimly circling the stuff without picking up even the ghost of a sign. There was ledgerock and brush, prickly pear and saguaro, around three sides and, on the fourth, a shelving drop that went guttering down into the blue-gray reaches of Needle Canyon. He guessed at once the vanished pair had pulled the shoes off their horses, but that didn't help him with so much sandstone around. It would be dark long before he could examine all that rock with the kind of care he'd need to pick up sign of barefoot horses. He did the next best thing and searched the shelves above Needle Canyon, finally forced to admit in bitter fury the pair had lost him.

His feuding passions boiled like pitch pine. Convinced by now he'd been deliberately doodled, he was like a wild man in his anger. Manergell had probably known all along where they were bound for, and he was minded in his outrage—in his terrible fear for Lucie—to go back to Barred Circle and tear the truth, piece by piece, from that gunhawk's lying throat.

The trouble was he realized, when he was able to think with any clarity, Manergell probably wouldn't be there now. Any work he put in at trailing might wind up just as these tracks had, and there was no time left to waste. They were moving in for the kill now and there was nothing left for a man to do but turn wolf like the rest of them.

He stared off in the direction of Swallowfork, giving no heed to the bay's restless stamping. He reckoned, as the crow flies, he was about ten miles from Forko Fox's headquarters, and at least four miles additional by the way he'd have to go. Thief River, on the other hand, was not a great deal farther. He stared at Samanthy's ears, scowling blackly. It went against all his training but there was, by grab, one thing he could do. He swung the bay around on the spot and struck out for Thief River.

It was a hell of a place, he thought, looking around at the scabrous buildings in the last red wink of the dying sun. The creaking shacks crouched like gray ghosts and no man showed, no horses either, though that sixth sense developed while he was marshal of Golden warned him he was being watched. Folding hands across the horn of Samanthy's Hamley he rode up to the largest house and stopped the horse with his knees. The place was in use; he could see the dark shapes of watching men through the wedged-open angle of the whoppyjawed door.

"If one of you jaspers will step out here and talk I've got a proposition that might be profitable for all of you."

A man's broad shape limped out onto the porch's warped planking and stood there a while without remark, darkly eyeing him.

"You the boss of this outfit?"

"Who wants to know?"

"My name is Rambo," Steve said, and caught

a faint shine of interest in the man's unwinking stare. "I want a herd of cattle moved—it might be two if the cards fall right."

The fellow on the porch took plenty of time turning it over, his fat little eyes all the while continuing to rummage Rambo's face.

"What's in it?"

"The second herd, if you can get it. If you can't, one thousand dollars when you've penned the first at Florence."

Several of the other shapes came out and stood loose grouped around the first. The broad man said, "Where do you fit into this?"

"I'm figuring to pull the Overpacks out of the hole they've been crowded into. If you don't want no part, now is the time to say so."

One black-hatted ruffian jutted his head forward and spat. "I rode fer that sonavabuck Deke one time. I say let 'em stew in their own juice!"

The broad-shouldered fellow, never taking his eyes off Rambo, said, "I've heard tell you're a tinbadge. So I'll ask you straight what you're fixin' to do."

"Run off a couple handfuls of cows but it begins to appear like I got into the wrong place. This ain't no chore that's been cut out for old ladies."

"You're pretty free with the gab," Broad Shoulders said, shoving the black-hatted rogue loose of his pistol. "How—"

"If you don't want the job, say so."

"Keep your cork in a minute. How big is these handfuls?"

"One I want delivered in Florence will be roughly around eight hundred head. Other bunch will probably run a lot closer to ten-twelve thousand." He said after a couple seconds of silence, "First bunch is gathered."

"Barred Circle?"

Rambo nodded. "You'll have to get them moving right away or you're no good to us. Girl owes the bank eight thousand on a note."

"Where's this second batch at?"

"Swallowfork."

A slow, queer gleam flickered back of the outlaw's eyes. "Man, you're bein' too generous with us." He held out his two hands. "Does them look like cat's paws?"

"This is no chickenyard deal—"

"You sure put your loop around that one. We don't mind a sniff of gunsmoke but, mister, we don't aim to pay for it!"

"How much do you want?"

"We'll take your thousand for movin' Barred Circle, plus another buck a head for every steer we land in the stock pens. If we engage to pull Swallowfork off your neck—"

"Never mind," Rambo said, "we'll let that part of it ride." He dug a roll of bills from his pocket and counted out five hundred. "You'll get the balance when the steers are delivered."

• • •

Night closed down like the jaws of a vise, catching Rambo at low ebb. He tried to persuade himself enlisting those outlaws—even in limited service—had been a shrewd move. It should catch Manergell and Anvil by surprise and force a redisposition of the men at their disposal. That should certainly be to the good and perhaps would prove so, but it wasn't finding Lucie.

He was in a foul mood when he got to Post Oak and tied Samanthy behind the Silver Trinket. He had no idea what had fetched him. There was an uneasy feeling at the back of his mind concerning Faron and that bank job George had hung on him, and it may have been this which had brought him into town. No one had to tell him this was not a good place for him.

He came out of the alley, still holding to the shadows, and hailed an old codger holding up the front of Kreighan's Furnishings, saying, "Got a match on you, pardner?"

The old man fished a couple from his vest and Rambo, taking them, said casually, "Bad thing, that killing at the bank the other day. How'd it happen?"

"How's anythin' happen? That batty Overpack kid! Droppin' a man over a piece of damn paper!"

The man hadn't shown any sign of recognition so Rambo, pressing his luck, said, "That all he got?"

"All he was after, accordin' to what they say. Asked ol' Rammickey to give him a look at this paper and beat him over the head with a pistol."

Fading back up the alley Rambo untied Samanthy and, keeping clear of the rubbish heaved behind these business places, moved along several doors before again seeking the street. This time he stayed in the saddle and, still following the uneasy hunch that was gnawing him, pulled up in the shadow of the assayer's closed office.

With hat tugged low he gave no mind to the passersby until a pair of gabbing cowhands breasted him heading for the open door of McAnelly's Pool Parlor. "Either of you gents tell me where I could locate the feller that runs the bank?"

Speaking almost in unison one said "Heaven" while his companion declared "Hell." Then, both laughing, the chunkier one said, "Misread his cards the other day and wound up takin' a trip with no ticket. Boss teller lives up at the end of this street—fourth shack on the left from the edge of the prairie."

Rambo thanked them and, turning down the next alley, moved again behind buildings till he reached the street's end. He still didn't know whereabouts this was taking him but, having come this far, decided to follow it through. Counting back from cropped grass he found the shack he was hunting had a light in the back and he got out of the saddle, leaving the bay on dropped reins.

He stepped onto the stoop and put his fist to the door. It was opened by a sandy-haired man in his shirtsleeves, disclosing a table and a stove. A pail of beer was on the table with a plate of crackers and some cheese. A peroxide blonde with big breasts and not much over them half turned in her chair to call, "Who is it, Alf?"

Rambo said to the man, "I'm looking into that killing you had at the bank the other day. I won't keep you long—just wanted to ask you a couple of questions."

After hesitating a moment the man came out and pulled the door shut. "What did you want to know?"

"I'd like to get a line on what happened. I understand Faron Overpack's been charged with the killing."

"Yeah. Well, there's not much I can tell you. Nobody actually saw it; they were in Rammickey's private office. The side door of the bank and the door of the office aren't more than about one long stride apart. I heard the old man's voice several times. Then a couple of bumps and a sound like somebody falling. When I looked round this guy was just going through the door."

"And that's all you saw?"

"Every last bit of it. I couldn't take any oath on

it one way or the other. I didn't see the fellow's face, or enough of him even to say how he was dressed. Except he had boots on. We were busier'n hell with the blower off. It was probably ten minutes before I got a chance to step in there—and I wouldn't have gone then except for the shots and all that racket outside. The old man had been beat over the head with a gun; that's what it looked like. He was dead when I found him."

"I understand the killer didn't lift any money."

"We couldn't tell what he took till we checked. So far as we could find he didn't actually take anything—"

"There was a note."

"We didn't have the note. It was taken up by Mr. Fox about a week ago. We were acting as his agent."

"I see," said Rambo thoughtfully. "If you couldn't say who the fellow was, how did the marshal get identification?"

"It seems when the killer got outside he grabbed the first horse he could get his hands on. Anvil James, who owned this horse, had just dismounted. The kid knocked him down and took off with the horse going hellity larrup. They exchanged several shots but James wasn't able to stop him."

"Then the identification rests on the word of—"

"Not entirely. He had a couple of his hands

185

with him. They allegedly saw Faron, too." He stood quiet for a moment. "I'm afraid that's all I can tell you; but if I were you, Rambo, I'd get out of this town pronto. And stay out."

It seemed to Rambo as he stepped off the stoop that what he had learned might tend to implicate Fox about as much as it did Anvil. It was the first direct evidence lending credence to Lucie's convictions. Fox had purchased Faron's note from the bank. It was enough to make a man do some strenuous thinking; for, if Fox had secretly bought up that note, might he not also have secretly been egging Anvil on, directing the operations which were slowly but inexorably pushing Barred Circle toward bankruptcy?

He certainly might. Steve, thinking back to that last talk he'd had with Fox, not only found it unsatisfactory but also more than a little suspicious. Particularly that sudden appearance of Anvil just when the talk had bade fair to get interesting. And, still more damning, the lack of any sound from the man, and Steve's finding of the fellow at Kelley's stable so shortly after.

On the other hand Fox had said from the start he was the obvious goat in this. Remembering the rancher's irascibility and unconcealable bitterness, Steve found it hard to believe the man had put on an act. As he had before, Steve came solidly again against the inescapable fact that if Fox was the polecat in the woodpile, he'd been treading on perilously thin ice hiring Rambo to bat around in circles like a chicken with its head off. And where was the profit? It would certainly have been cheaper and a thousand times less risky, if Fox were afraid of Rambo, to have Steve taken care of with a bushwhacker's bullet.

It was far more likely to be Anvil as Fox maintained. The ramrod had an almost perfect screen to work behind. The country had Fox pegged for an unscrupulous grasping range baron. Every move Anvil made was traced right back to orders from Fox—and someway Anvil had found out about that gold, about the clues to its whereabouts being on Barred Circle . . . on the part, like enough, which Anvil had himself once owned.

Since Lucie's brother, of Steve's own knowledge, could not possibly have been within miles of the bank at the time someone's gun had beaten Rammickey to death, the most logical killer was Anvil himself who could easily have made it after quitting Raid's Store while Steve had been packing Faron Overpack home. And he had been there—with two hands—in time to hang the frame on Faron. And, unless Steve's hunch was wide of the mark, one of those hands had been the storekeeping fat man.

It added up. He wanted Faron out of the way. Convinced by that whaling the kid's hoof-kinked mind would never disgorge the location of that stone horse head, he wanted Faron out of the way so that Lucie, as heir apparent, would stand defenseless in possession of his goal—the great Barred Circle.

Rambo stopped with deepening breath twenty strides from Samanthy, startled mind set whirling with another recollection. That yellow-booted gunslick had hinted this noon what the score was with Anvil—more than hinted. When Steve had guessed that Lucie's abduction was likely intended to pull them into a trap, Manergell had said the ramrod's probable intention was to force the girl into marriage.

Now, in view of the way those tracks had vanished, it seemed the logical shortcut to everything the bald-headed vinegarroon was after. If the gold was there marriage would give him that too; Barred Circle was patented land and could not be invaded for the staking of claims.

A disturbed bottle clanked against tin cans to the right of him and Rambo, ducking instinctively with hand flying hipward, saw a darker blotch in the murk between shacks—the shape of a man who now called: *"Rambo! Hold it!"*

With naked steel in his hand Rambo crouched there, hard staring. The crash of his heart against ribs was like thunder. Recognition of the voice finally ate through his caution and, lowering the gun, he stepped into the alley to face Forko Fox.

17

"Man," Fox said, "are you crazy?"

In the dark his low voice was harsh with suppressed violence. "For a man with five hundred dollars on his scalp you show damn poor judgment sticking your nose into this place!"

"What about that government tin—"

"This is no time for jokes! Ain't a man in this country puts any stock in that now—thank God I stumbled onto you! Where's your horse?"

Rambo pointed.

"Too far," Fox growled. "Someone's tipped the marshal. We'll have to cut and run for it."

Rambo shoved him back into the deeper shadows. "No use you getting tied into this—"

The Swallowfork owner thinly said in bleak outrage: "When a man hires on with me I stand behind him all the way."

Rambo scowled a moment, listening; twisted his face an inch and whistled. "You damn fool!" Fox swore, grabbing hold of him. Rambo shook off his grip and stepped away and Fox, still wild, said in a tone he must have rolled first in sand, "Didn't I just get through telling you George knows you're up here? He's got this whole end of town blocked off—"

He stopped talking, looking astonished, as Samanthy—head high to keep the reins out from under him—came up through the shadows and started nuzzling Rambo's shoulder. "Neat," Fox said, "but no good to you now. We'll have to crawl—"

"I may come to that," Steve answered, "but I'm not about to do any crawling right now. Where's your mount?"

"Out in those China—"

The crash of a gun ripped through Fox's words, the unseen snarl of its tunneling lead sweeping past them so narrowly Samanthy slammed both hind feet at the stars, squealing wickedly. All across the back lots muzzle light started winking and Rambo, crowding Fox ahead of him, hauled the gelding into the street and hopped onto him.

Fox darted into a black murk of umbrella trees and came out mounted. But, in the fraction of time it had taken him to do so, the men bent on cutting Rambo down had sprung from cover and were now closing in, firing rapidly. They were appearing on both sides of the deserted street now and a third unit, bellied down in the dirt, were opening up with rifles from behind the grass hummocks where the street sheered off into open range. Through that deadly curtain of lead Rambo wheeled the laid-back ears of his bay straight into the lighted heart of town, the ranchman pelting beside him under quirt and spur.

It seemed incredible so many shots could be fired without emptying both saddles. Steve, riding like an Apache, was snapping an occasional return shot high from under Samanthy's out-stretched neck, but the Swallowfork owner's ingrained pride would not permit him to seek such undignified shelter and he rode with a calvaryman's poker-stiff posture.

In this fashion they swerved abruptly left between buildings, cutting down the racket of exploding firearms and filling the roundabout night with hoof pound. "Which way?" Rambo called, and Fox shouted: "Barred Circle!" and turned his horse dead away from it, thundering across Fremont; Rambo, puzzled, riding hard in his wake. Down another black passage between buildings they tore and out onto the range in a dead run for the hills.

They put two miles between themselves and town in this manner before Fox pulled his heaving mount to a stop. "That will bollix them for a bit, I think—long enough to get us clear, anyway."

"If you were recognized back there, this business isn't going to win any friends for you."

Fox's chin jutted. "I know my friends. I don't have any in that place—Anvil has managed to make damned sure of that much."

They sat in silence for awhile then, listening through the blowing of their horses for sound of pursuit. Rambo was about to put a number of pointed questions when the owner of Swallow-fork abruptly said, "I don't think you're going to like this and, in a way, I can't much blame you. I'm not satisfied myself but I feel bound to admit I think I've found your man."

"Man?" Rambo peered at him stupidly, his mind too filled with other things overlayed by his worries and very real concern for Lucie to catch the drift of the rancher's words. "What man?"

"That fellow you said had fetched you up out of Pecos. You'll recall we decided if the fellow lived around here it would have to be someone who'd been away a spell. I have checked and double-checked and, bad as I hate to put anything else on him, he's the only one I've been able to locate who was out of this country at about the right time."

Rambo said through locked jaws, "Who is he?"

"Faron Overpack."

Feeling more bone-weary than he had in months, Forko Fox rode into Swallowfork headquarters shortly after ten to find the horse trap empty and no men in sight anywhere. All the buildings lay shrouded in darkness. Dirty Shirt, he reckoned, was probably snoring in the cookshack. He damned Anvil roundly for pulling all the hands away from the place; and unsaddled his horse and turned it loose to roll in one of the big heavy stock pens. He fetched an armful of hay and a coffee can of rolled oats (being privately of the opinion that whole oats were wasteful). He thrust a hand in the trough to make sure the horse had water. Then, sighing irascibly, he headed for the house.

That had been a near thing in town and it had shaken him more than he had at the time realized. He could feel the shake in his knees just recalling the angry whine of those blue whistlers droning past them. It had been a long while since anyone had turned a belching firearm at Forko Fox. He didn't like even the memory of it. George was getting damned careless what kind of timber he took for deputies.

He let himself into the house and shot the bolt after him, a thing he very seldom did. He found the living-room lamp and put a match to it, turning up the wick after resettling the big glass chimney as though subconsciously feeling the need of bringing his surroundings into clearer perspective. He pulled off his coat and laid it over a chair arm and got a fresh Havana.

It was while he was tipped forward, igniting it from the heat rising out of the lamp's chimney, that Fox realized abruptly he was not alone in this room.

He gave no sign of the alarm roaring through him, no evidence of pounding pulses. He puffed the cigar into life, made sure it was burning evenly, before he stepped back with a casual turn of his head which discovered the man in front of the horsehair sofa. He saw the yellow boots first and then he found the hands, both empty.

Barred Circle's new man grinned. "A little bit early but 'Merry Christmas.'"

"What are you doing here, Gellerman? I thought I made it clear that you—"

"You made a lot of things clear but you forgot to tell me what Anvil was after. I'll be more valuable to you now. A lot more valuable," he said, smiling broadly.

"I made you a price—"

Manergell brushed that aside. "Let's put the cards on the table. You think there's gold on that place."

"You're confusing me with Anvil."

"Oh no I'm not." The gunhawk's grin stretched tight and cold. "And the price has gone up, Forko. You can cut out the play-actin'. That roll you gave me at Thief River was down-payment on a dead man. What I'm offerin' you now is silence."

After Yellow Boots said that both stood utterly still while the clock on the mantel swung its pendulum six times. Fox rasped, "You're crazy!"

"I don't think so," Manergell said. "If getting a certain party killed is worth two grand on top of the thousand I get for watching him, keeping my lip buttoned should be worth a sight more."

The ranchman's face stayed blank as a poker chip. "I don't blame any man for trying to better himself, but you're on the wrong foot. Anvil only thinks there might be gold on that spread. He'll probably never know now because the one fellow who might have substantiated his theories has disappeared."

"You're talkin' of Overpack?"

"Overpack's rattlebrained cub. Anvil gave the kid a beating and he dug for the tules." Fox spread his hands and dropped them. "There you have it, Gellerman. When I hire a man I aim to go the whole distance with him. But you can't get blood from a turnip, and that's the size of it."

Yellow Boots grinned. "You're a pretty slick article. So here's my proposition and I ain't figurin' to repeat it. You'll cut me in for a third of whatever you two get out of this, with another three grand put in my hand right now for earnest, or I'll go do some chinnin' with Rambo."

Fox's bone-hard glance roved over the gun fighter's face and he curled thin lips with ineffable contempt. "All right. You've made your bluff. Now get the hell out of here."

The gunhawk's own lips came off his teeth and he said, "Still the play-actin' maker of big gestures." Behind their squeezed-down lids his eyes turned flat as fish scales. The .44 at his groin was suddenly naked in his fist. "All you're hopin' to get is a look at my back and that is one thing, Forko, you ain't ever goin' to have. You got a safe over there tucked away behind that bookcase. Start twirlin' the knob before I change that pretty face to where your own Maw wouldn't know it."

The ranchman's eyes were wild with hate but there wasn't enough grit in his craw to withstand the baleful stare of that leveled sixshooter. With his cheeks gray as ashes he pulled the bookcase out of the way and knelt before the black face of his castiron strongbox.

When its inches-thick door swung silently open Manergell showed his twisted grin and said, "Remember, three full thousand. When you get it counted out get a pen and a piece of paper and put me down for a full third share of whatever you sidewinders take from Barred Circle."

196

18

After the ranchman left Rambo had no idea how long he sat hunched there in the seat of his saddle with his turbulent thoughts wheeling around Fox's disclosure. Faron Overpack was Kramer! What a fool he had been not to grasp the truth sooner. He had the build, good looks and everything. Steve could see it just as plain as he could see Samanthy's ears in these down-slanting shafts of the late-rising moon. Clear as crystal he recalled the kid's uneasy glances, the look of his frightened face when he'd chopped off that talk about the lost bonanza. No wonder he had cleared out when he'd realized Steve's identity!

The memory of Steve's dead sister came to haunt him with reproachful eyes. He heard her voice in the run of the wind, a pitiful cry rising out of her grave, demanding to know why he didn't avenge the honor Faron Overpack had dragged through the muck like a calf at a rope's end.

Lucie's brother!

Rambo bitterly cursed the knowledge Fox had given him. He lashed Samanthy with the reins and almost instantly pulled him up again, knowing in his heart this was a thing he'd got to face. He couldn't ride away from it, couldn't leave this country. He'd found something here and it wasn't a thing he could find someplace else. Not down the trail or over the hills but only on Barred Circle. He looked a long while into the face of the dreams he'd built up these last days and his guts turned cold with the hopelessness of them, with the hell-spawned anguish of having to come to such a choice.

He felt a touch of hope when he remembered Faron wasn't available but he put that hope away from him, knowing this wasn't a thing any man with a code could sidestep. The issue was plain. Nor was he hypocrite enough to hide the truth behind his training. Those years he'd spent in meditation and study, those nights he'd walked with the Lord had not stopped him from taking up this vengeance trail when he had learned of Della's seduction and suicide.

His own flesh and blood! Could he do less for it now?

In a paroxysm of despair he lashed the bay again, blindly driving it over the trail Fox had taken.

In town, after the collapse of the trap set for Rambo, the crooked nosed marshal used his tongue like a whip on the volunteer deputies who had so miserably failed to live up to their boasts and his own expectations. "What the hell were you using—blank cartridges?" He flayed them with the filth of the back rooms and brothels. He called them puking whores' sons and sent them blasphemously after horses; and one surly fellow, who swung round to snarl back at him, he knocked in the head with a swipe of his gun-barrel.

Only five reassembled, the toughest of the breed that hung around the dives of Post Oak. Ruffians who would follow his orders without question—kill-hungry triggers bought with the silence of the star Fox had furnished.

When all were in their saddles he said, looking them over, "We're takin' that bastard wherever we find him and we're not fetchin' back anything but his scalp."

Samanthy drank from the spring without hurry, now and again pulling up his bay head to sniff the air, while Rambo stood in deep grass at his side, surveying with bitter eyes the feeble glimmer of light which came from behind the drawn blind in Fox's living-room. All the rest of the house and the other buildings were dark and Steve was wondering, now he'd got here, what fool impulse could have brought him.

A frog croaked somewhere inside the rustle of the cottonwoods. The night was cool but there was sweat on Rambo's cheeks and the back of his shirt was damp with it, a clammy feeling dampness like the squirm in his gutless belly. What good could it do to see Fox again? The man had made his report according to his promise and bothering him again would not change the information he had given with extreme reluctance.

Of course he'd been reluctant! There could be no advantage to Fox in Faron's death—everyone would think Fox was back of it no matter whose hand actually struck the kid down. It was the measure of the ranchman's innocence and the thorough honesty of his good faith that, knowing this, he could still keep his promise and give Steve the unpalatable facts.

He shook his head and scowled unhappily. Forko Fox had no reason for desiring Faron dead. Unless . . .

Rambo, staring at the light showing back of those drawn window shades, ridiculed the fantastic notions which his feverish mind, in its efforts to free him from the horns of his dilemma, sought to insinuate into his thinking. He had but two real choices—either to go after Lucie's brother or to let the kid go. In this country a man killed snakes no matter what it cost him.

Talking further with Fox wouldn't change this.

He got back into the saddle, darkly thinking of Raid's Store, and was about to rein Samanthy in that general direction when, through the night's cool stillness, he caught the skreak of an opening door. There was only one door on this ranch wailed like that, the door that let into that room with the lamp. The one he'd himself used the last time he'd been here—the time Forko Fox, peering out, had seen Anvil.

Something made him hold back, screened by the cottonwoods, hearing boots and voices. The talk was too low for him to distinguish actual words though he decided it was mostly being done by one man; by someone he should place, he thought. He guessed that they were coming around the back of the house, and waited.

With narrowed stare he watched the moonlit corner. The pair walked into view, one of them leading a saddle horse which now, with a saturnine laugh, he got onto. Twisting around he said, "I'll take care of him—partner. And I'll be takin' that filly off your hands, also."

Still chuckling, Manergell reined his horse across the slope.

Long moments after the gun fighter's hoof sound had faded Fox was still by the corner of the house staring after him. Rambo had no key that would unlock the man's thoughts nor any means, either, of interpreting what he'd heard. But the mere fact that Manergell and Fox were acquainted was sufficiently disturbing to upset all former notions.

Was Manergell playing both ends from the middle? Was he taking pay from Anvil and taking money from Fox as well, or was he kingpin in

this deal as Steve had once before halfway suspected? It might be some business deal in horses
which had brought the fellow here to see Fox. In
that case he'd probably said "pardner" . . .

Rambo brushed thought aside as Fox, abruptly
straightening, whirled away from the moonlit
wall. He wasn't going into the house, he was
heading for one of the stock pens. He broke into
a run and Rambo's eyes narrowed as he saw
the man snatch a rope from a saddle and slide
through the bars of the stoutest corral.

He reappeared in a moment, coming out with
a horse which he hurriedly saddled; and now
Rambo's thoughts turned his face grim as death.
Fox ducked into a shed and returned lugging a
rifle. He mounted and, reining the horse between
buildings, gained the slope over which the derby-
hatted gunhawk had so recently departed. Near
its crest he paused for what seemed an eternity,
finally disappearing.

When Steve reached that point he saw, off
to the south perhaps a couple of miles, a faint
tracery of haze which he took erroneously to
be the dust of the departing gun fighter. He was
much more interested in the shape speeding north
for this, a great deal nearer and quite plain in the
moonglow, was obviously Fox. The man was
heading in the direction of the camp where Brick
had died. Rambo waited five more minutes and
then put Samanthy after him.

Moonlight distorts things, makes a mockery of distance. Steve, knowing this, was careful not to crowd the man too close. He didn't think Fox's destination was likely to be that linecamp. Considering Manergell's visit, and those laughing words he'd thrown at Fox before departing, Steve had a pretty shrewd hunch what was taking Fox north. So long as there was moonlight Rambo was content to let the man hold his lead, not worrying when occasionally he dropped clean out of sight.

He had it figured this would prove to be a ride of some duration. When Fox passed the deserted linecamp two hours later without stopping Rambo nodded, confident now his hunch had been a good one.

Gradually now the man ahead was swinging east toward the barren waste of rock and shale through which Steve, in the afternoon, had unsuccessfully followed Anvil. He saw Fox drop between low hills and pulled up for a bit to let Samanthy blow. For the past hour the pace had been an easy lope and Steve didn't think Fox suspected he was followed, but there was always the chance the man might get a change of horses and, if that happened and the man put on a burst of speed, there seemed a very good chance that Steve would wind up losing him. If he got into that lava and ledgerock . . .

Already Fox's dust was beginning to thin.

Steve pushed Samanthy, presently pausing again to take hurried bearings. Ever more surely the course of Swallowfork's owner was swinging in the direction of a blue haze off yonder which Steve deduced to be Needle Canyon.

Raid's Store came into his mind again yet he was reluctant to believe this was Fox's destination. The tracks Steve had followed had not gone into the canyon; at least he had found no evidence to prove it.

But Fox's actions from the first had seemed keyed to Manergell's visit and Steve was betting his all that Fox was making this trip because of something the derby-hatted gun fighter had said. He was bound to believe it had to do with that "filly" Tax Manergell had said he would take off Fox's hands. To Steve that term was synonymous with Lucie.

Had they dared hold Lucie at Raid's Store? It seemed extremely unlikely. Yet it was becoming ever more increasingly obvious that Fox was bound for that lava and ledgerock where the tracks of Anvil's splayfooted dun had vanished. This was final proof to Steve that Fox was hurrying to the girl. And beyond the lava lay Needle Canyon.

Memory can play queer tricks on a man. Trying to plumb it is like trying to dredge the ocean deeps with a fish net, yet sometimes it turns up things of its own volition as Steve's did then.

No dust showed ahead now. Fox was on ledgerock. This could mean the ranchman had discovered he was being followed and, with sufficient lead, was planning to lose pursuit as Anvil had lost Steve earlier. It could mean something entirely different—even ambush. If Fox thought Manergell was on his trail there was no telling what he would do.

Steve had to gamble. And it was while he was sitting there, trying to make up his mind, that he chanced to glance around and discovered the dust behind him. There was too much of it to be made by one horse. Only one thing was certain: These were no friends of his!

He whirled Samanthy to the right and sent him up a limestone draw thickly screened with oak and manzanita. The gelding's hoofs kicked up sound from the thin covering of earth and then he ran onto soft ground, clattered across a dry wash and came out above the foliage into a crazy landscape of gigantic rocks which had fallen in some prehistoric time from the red cliffs towering high above them.

Rambo swung north there, angling north by east as they tore over dry grass to thread the maze of boulders on a tangent that should bring them to the eastern end of Needle Canyon. What Steve had remembered was that abandoned Barred Circle linecamp he had passed the afternoon he had packed Faron Overpack home from Raid's

Store. It was the one place no one would ever think to look for Lucie. And now he remembered something else. *He hadn't ever told Fox he'd come into this country from Pecos.*

Out of the welter of his thoughts a lot of other things came clear, and one of them was Tax Manergell. Rambo's lips thinned with hate and for the first time since he'd had him he raked Samanthy's flanks with his spurs.

The moon was down when the bay carried Rambo up an eroded slope which came out on the bench leading into Needle Canyon. Too dark to see Raid's Store, but the black mass of trees which surrounded it he could pick from the star-splattered blackness beyond. To the right, in trees also and more completely concealed in the thick curdled gloom, was the Barred Circle linecamp, less than half a mile off.

He was in a real sweat to put his hunch to the test and to get—if she were there—Lucie out of the place; but he knew better than to rush the place blindly. Having gone this far Anvil wouldn't be fool enough to leave her unguarded.

The night was filled with murmurs and a faint ground breeze, curling down from the higher rimrock, fluttered the scarf at Rambo's throat and laved the gelding's lathered hide. Samanthy swelled his barrel to blow but a constriction of Rambo's knees curbed the impulse.

The dark was always deepest before dawn Steve

remembered with his head cocked, anxiously listening through the pant of the animal's breathing. He thought to catch the rumor of traveling horses but he could not be certain and, while he was trying, booted feet moved across the warped planks of Raid's Store.

Steve dropped out of the saddle, matching stealth with stealth. Whoever that was they could hardly have failed to hear Samanthy's approach. It didn't seem too likely Fox would have gotten here ahead of him. That was probably one of Anvil's crew, perhaps the ramrod himself creeping up through the darkness with a cocked gun in hand.

It wasn't fear that held Steve scarce-breathing in his tracks. Maybe it was in a way, but it wasn't personal fear, not fright for what might happen to himself. Fear, rather, of what might be in store for Lucie if he, by one wrong choice or blundering move, was prevented from getting her out of this. It was hard to think with his heart banging that way.

If he tackled the fellow and there were other bravos around they might slip the girl away before he could prevent them. He had no real proof she was being held at the linecamp and if he didn't take care of this fellow right now it was a foregone conclusion the man would set a trap for him. If he tried to move Samanthy the man would hear and take a gun to him, and what good would he be to Lucie if he reached her without a horse?

Time was of the essence and time was running out.

How fast it was slipping through his fingers he suddenly realized when, twisting his head, he heard what he had been scared he would. That was hoof sound, all right. Though still far away it was coming up fast—and not just one horse, either.

Sweat cracked through the skin on Steve's neck. His mouth was so dry he couldn't even swallow. Turned desperate—near panicked—he was about to swing into the saddle again when a harsh whisper leaped from the murk to his left. "Forko?"

A whisper is a voice disembodied. Steve's thoughts jumped around like frogs' legs in a skillet but he couldn't pin it down, couldn't tag the man's identity. He was sure it was the fellow he had heard at Raid's Store but that was far as he could take it. His heart was hammering his ribs so hard he couldn't even hear the hoof sound now, and he knew if he didn't say something quick the man who had spoken was going to start throwing lead.

"For Christ sake, Forko, can't you hear them goddam horses?"

The man's jumpity voice came out of the felted black not six feet from Steve's elbow. They

208

glimpsed each other at the very same moment; but Steve—now free of his paralysis—was able coolly to calculate the one thin chance finally shoved his way by fate.

The strain-cracked nerves which had pushed the man into unguarded speech had dropped the last link into place and Rambo saw in this moment that he could never have killed Faron. When the chips were down he couldn't have given up Lucie for an oath made to a dead woman's memory. Pride had shaped that thought and God had stripped the pride from him by showing him how completely he'd been played for a sucker.

He said, "Drop that gun, Allison."

19

Lucie's range boss fired from the hip, triggering frantically—but Steve wasn't where he had been when he'd spoken. It was too dark for this kind of thing even in close quarters; but Steve's descending gunbarrel, though it missed the treacherous Allison's head, caught the fellow at the base of the throat and he went down with a broken collar bone, screaming.

Steve was onto him at once with both knees, heavily, gun swinging wickedly. Allison wilted. Rambo gagged him and tied him, dragged him back under the trees and there left him, diving for Samanthy, desperately hauling himself into the saddle with the horse already running and the sounds of those others lifting into wild thunder.

Steve, whirling his head toward the Barred Circle linecamp, put him into a dead run, thankful in this murk the big bay was sure-footed. He couldn't see ten yards ahead of them but he heard the skreak of the thrown-open door and Anvil's panic-tight voice in a thin bleat demanding, "Forko! Forko?—is that you, Forko?" and drove the horse straight at him.

A lance of flame gouted out of the dark and Steve put two slugs squarely into the flash of it and heard Anvil yell as he leaped from the saddle. Anvil fired again and then Steve crashed into him, carrying them both to the ground in a wild thrashing tangle.

Rambo tried to find the man's head with his gunbarrel. Anvil's gun roared again, the flash of it blinding Steve, searing his cheek with its grains of hot powder. Then Steve's weapon connected and the man went limp under him.

Rambo clawed to his feet and ran into the door and picked himself up and got his hands on it this time. "Lucie!" he cried, panting. "Lucie—you in there?"

He heard a cloth-muffled whimper, a scrape of sound from the floor. He struck a match, going in, and saw her lashed to a bench. He cut the ropes, took the gag from her mouth. He ached to take her into his arms but there was no time for it. "Quick," he gruffed—"where's Anvil's horse?"

She had difficulty forming words, couldn't make them intelligible yet; seemed hardly able to keep her legs under her but, leaning heavily on him, she got him around to the rear of the place. He found the splayfooted dun with another Swallowfork bronc in a kind of a shed built against the shack's back.

Both were saddled. Knowing the dun for a horse with bottom, he slipped the bridle over its head and tightened the saddle's cinches. He boosted Lucie aboard and whistled up Samanthy. "Can you manage to stay on?"

"Yes," she said hoarsely.

Even now streaks of gray were breaking through the eastern blackness and the avalanche of hoof sound was become a hard drumming roar as it swept out of the trees and howled on across the clearing where Rambo had tangled with Allison.

"Let's go," Steve said, swinging onto Samanthy. It was a cinch they'd be heard soon as those horsebackers stopped but there was no help for that. No good trying to hide from them, either; in half an hour it would be light. Their only chance lay in running—in the hearts and guts and sinews of these two willing horses under them.

"Who is it?" Lucie asked.

"Swallowfork toughs or a posse from Post Oak. Fox is probably with them—you were right about him all along. I've been a fool," he answered gruffly, and was grateful for her silence.

Punching the empties from his pistol, he thumbed fresh loads into its cylinder, praying that for once he might be right in the guess he was making. He kept Samanthy going straight north till they got out of the timber.

It was getting light fast by that time, and when they'd put the last of the trees behind they were in shale country again with barren hills thrusting skyward all across the gray horizon. Still moving north Rambo turned the gelding's nose into the west on a tangent which he hoped would intersect the Barred Circle trail herd which that crew from Thief River should have well along by this time.

Overtaking that herd was their one slim chance by Steve's reckoning. Plainly Allison had left it to report what was happening and, save for running into Rambo, would have done so. It was Steve's intention—if he could do it—to slam Fox's crew right into the guns of those owlhooters.

They were crawling through a region of fantastic rocks that was like nothing Steve Rambo had ever seen before. This was an up-and-down country pitched crazily on end like something seen under the influence; the rocks were gray against a bleached yellow soil that looked jaundiced as the matter squeezed out of a puffed-up sore. The rocks were everywhere about them, gray and huge and ugly as a group of slaughtered mammoths, and through some indecipherable thought process Steve was reminded of Dante's Inferno.

Bone weary he was and too bitterly discouraged any longer to conceal it. His gut felt like it had been hauled through a knothole. His red-veined stare and irascible features, discernible to the girl when he looked back across his shoulder, were too bleak to be dissembled, too deeply etched with foreboding to be viewed with aught but dread. Samanthy moved now at a stumbling walk, too spent to pick his feet up, and a mile behind a powdery haze still clung to their back-trail with the devil's persistence. Yet, strangely, she was able to manage a wan smile until he asked out of the sunblasted silence if she had heard anything further about or from Faron.

She closed her eyes then and her hands gripped the saddle horn so tight her knuckles whitened. "Buried under the floor of that shack where you found me."

"They killed him?"

Her eyes came open. "They tortured him till his heart quit. They wouldn't believe he didn't know where the Dutchman's mine is hidden."

Rambo told her then why he'd come into this country—about Deuce Kramer and his sister. "Fox told me last night Faron was Kramer—"

"He lied!"

"I know. You had his number. He's been back of your troubles all along. And back of mine."

"You mean . . . your sister?"

Rambo nodded. "When Anvil, Colorado and myself rode in that day to report Brick's killing, I knew Fox was a frightened man. But he took me in, cunningly turning it to his own advantage, making me believe it was his range boss he was scared of." He repeated what Fox had told him. "The bill of goods he sold me was tricked out so plausibly I couldn't accept the things you told me about him. He'd been shrewd enough to disarm me in advance."

"Yes," Lucie said out of the hoof-pocked quiet, "he could put it on or turn it off. I can't blame you, Steve. After all, you didn't know him. You were a stranger here and he can be very convincing." She asked after a moment, "What woke you up?"

"He did. Last night. After I lost Anvil's tracks I rode into town and had a talk with that teller. Leaving his place I ran into Fox. I thought that was a bit fortuitous. He said I'd been seen, that George was laying a trap for me; and right about then the guns started barking. He grabbed hold of me but I shook him off and we climbed on our horses. They had us nearly surrounded and there was a heap of lead thrown but we got out of it— Fox riding stiff as a colonel of cavalry, and never a scratch. I thought that was queerer.

"I got to thinking of your remarks then, of all the things that have been happening at and to Barred Circle. All of them tied up with Swallow-fork. I worked over Fox's story and did some thinking about Anvil, and that yellow-booted gunhawk you hired on the other day. I knew there was something lurking in the deal I couldn't get hold of; I was pretty well convinced Fox was about what you said he was. Then he came out with that crack about Faron.

"I couldn't think straight. I left him. I was too wild to think of anything but killing Faron—it was like a swig of pulque hitting the bottom of an empty belly. Then I remembered you. I knew I couldn't do it—not right away, of course. It kind of crept up on me gradual. I wanted to talk with Fox again. There was something burning in the back of my mind. I rode out there and found Fox talking with Manergell. That tied him up as the big skunk in your woodpile; and then I remembered what he had said.

"When he told me he'd got a line on my man I was thinking of something else and didn't catch on right away. I said, 'What man?' And Fox said, 'That fellow you said had fetched you up out of Pecos.' Then he told me it was Faron Overpack. But when I saw him and Yellow Boots chinning in the moonlight, I remembered that and knew I'd never said a single word to him about Pecos. Things began to add up, and then Manergell took off and Fox, as soon as he was gone, ran and saddled up a horse. It was while I was following him it all fell together and I knew he was the man Della'd known as Deuce Kramer."

After a while Lucie said, "Do you think the Lost Dutchman is behind what he's been up to?"

"Behind his attempts to take over or break Barred Circle? No. I think the gold was Anvil's angle . . . maybe Anvil's and the marshal's. I'll not say Fox wouldn't be averse to grabbing it, but I don't think he believes it can be found. I think his goal from the start has been power; it's the land he wants, all the land in this country. I think it's become a mania with him. He can't stand the thought of playing second fiddle to anyone."

The sun climbed higher, beating down with an insensate fury on this wilderness of rock and sand. No green here but the waxen pads of stunted pear. The tag-end of God's work, worthless scrap left in hand when on the seventh day He'd rested. Piled desolation at the rim of the world.

Its blinding light was sheerest agony to scalded eyes. It split puffed lips and boiled up from the slants of rock like devil fire, rasping parched throats that were as dry as ashes. And all the while, like a creeping monster, that thin pale haze to the rear inched nearer with the inevitability of foretold doom.

Rambo, acknowledging he'd overshot the herd or that those masterless rogues from Thief River had made off with it, knew they could not hold out much longer. Samanthy, game to the core, had used the stored reserves of his strength and moved now at a drunken stagger, head down, eyes glazing, as hopeless a caricature of his once proud self as the distorted shadow which lurched at his side. His breath was a ghastly wheeze, almost a rattle.

Anvil's dun, under Lucie, having had some chance to rest, might perhaps keep going for another half hour. It might be enough if Steve could find the right place.

Another twist of his head picked up the pursuit less than half a mile behind. Like banshees they shimmered and wavered back there in the curl of the heat against the bright brassy sky. Now, against rock, they lost their black blobby look and became grinning ogres on horseback. Six of them he counted and made out Crooked Nose George and Fox in the lead. Their mounts had dropped to a walk but there weren't any of them staggering.

Lucie's eyes met his and Steve snarled back a groan. For it was hard, bitter hard, grasping now all she could mean to him to have to put her love away and let her go from him untold. Yet it were better so. Only selfishness, if she won free, would shackle her to a dead man's memory.

He saw a shape of land which might serve his purpose. The spine of a ridge ran across the horizon, bleakly gray as the upthrust slabs of furnace rock about them, shutting out of their sight all that lay beyond it. And, stabbing into the glare, thrusting out of the shale littered slope climbing up to it, were three black buttes crouched like half-asleep sentinels.

He reined the staggering Samanthy toward these, desperately afraid the bay couldn't make it. But though he stumbled twice and almost went down the horse someway carried Steve into their shade. Lucie, on her sweat-darkened dun, was close on his right as they passed between the second and third buttes within a stone's throw of the hogback's crest. Rambo, taking one final backward look, saw Fox with George's toughs hardly a quarter mile back.

"Keep going," Rambo grated, dropping off with his rifle. He didn't give her a chance to argue. "Somewhere beyond this ridge you'll hit the road to Florence—take it and keep riding!" He slapped the dun on the rump with his hat.

But she wheeled him back.

Rambo cursed. It was all he could do.

He ran to an outjutting spur of the butte's base, tugged the brim of his hat down across his eyes and climbed into a crevice which he figured would give him clear view of George's crew. It did. But, before he could bring up his rifle, lead chipped rock two inches from his face and it hadn't come from any of that climbing bunch with Fox!

He heard the whang of the heavy Sharps and, wheeling his head for a look behind him, saw Manergell crouched high up on the third butte. He knew the man by his hat—about all he could see behind the glint of that buffalo gun. Even as Steve looked the heavy weapon coughed again and something burnt like jerked rope across the side of his neck, unsettling his precarious foothold and toppling him.

The drop was only ten feet but it shook the breath out of him, spraddling him out like a steer for the branding. He could feel the hot seep of blood on his shoulder; caught Lucie's whimpering cry—the spiteful crack of her saddle gun.

She missed but Steve didn't. As Manergell whirled to face the girl Rambo's slug took the outlaw between exposed shoulders and knocked him off the butte screaming.

But Fox's men were warned. Steve heard the pounding of hoofs—they seemed to be all around him; and there were shouts and cursing, a building racket of gunfire. And out of this uproar a black horse and rider slammed around the butte's base, the man triggering wildly.

Steve fired from the hip and saw the black horse go down, but the man sprang clear, doing a crazy thing then. He let go of his gun as though the touch of it burned him, crying, "No—no! Don't kill me—don't shoot; I'm finished," and put both empty shaking hands above his head.

It was Forko Fox but Steve had hard work recognizing this disheveled, dust-smeared, goggle-eyed wretch for the fastidious, suave and plausible cowman who had schemed to smash Barred Circle and make himself master of this mountain empire. He looked a frightened little man when a group of hard-faced brush-clawed riders choused what was left of George's Post Oakers into the picture.

Rambo felt suddenly light in the head. The

change from sure death to complete victory was too abrupt, too overwhelming. He couldn't grasp where these grinning fellows had come from. The broad shape of their spokesman, doffing his hat out of deference to Lucie, said to Steve, "Hope you ain't sore about us bustin' up your fun, boss. We was restin' that herd just across the next ridge. We knowed it wasn't none of our put-in—"

"You cut it pretty close," Rambo said, "but I'm not kicking. Any time you get fed up with crime and can settle down to humdrum work there'll be jobs for every one of you—"

"On Barred Circle," Lucie said, breaking into it.

"Why, ma'am, we're apt to be around," the fellow grinned; and then, to Steve: "What you wantin' us to do with this here bunch of short-horns?"

"Guess you better push them along with the rest of our stuff; the law over at Florence will probably be glad to buy them. None of your boys wanted in that neighborhood, are they?"

Broad Shoulders shook his head. "What about this 'un?" He jerked a thumb at the Swallowfork owner.

Rambo rested a long look on the ranchman, remembering Della, remembering other things, too. At last he said, "That one's just a coyote got up in fox's clothing. I don't expect it'll fetch much but you can take it along with the rest if you want to."

He turned his back on Fox then and walked over to Lucie.